Also by Suzanne Fisher Staples

The Green Dog
Shiva's Fire
Dangerous Skies
Haveli
Shabanu
The House of Djinn

UNDER THE

PERSIMMON TREE

SUZANNE FISHER STAPLES

SQUARE FISH

FARRAR STRAUS GIROUX

SQUARE
FISH

An Imprint of Macmillan

Square Fish and the Square Fish logo are trademarks of
Macmillan and are used by Farrar Straus Giroux under
license from Macmillan.

Originally published in the United States by
Farrar Straus Giroux
Square Fish logo designed by Filomena Tuosto
Designed by Barbara Grzeslo
First Square Fish Edition: April 2008
11 13 15 17 16 14 12 10
mackids.com

AR: 5.9 / F&P: Y / LEXILE: 1010L

Library of Congress Cataloging-in-Publication Data
Staples, Suzanne Fisher.
  Under the persimmon tree / Suzanne Fisher Staples.
    p. cm.
  Summary: During the 2001 Afghan War, the lives of Najmah,
a young refugee from Kunduz, Afghanistan, and Nusrat, an
American-Muslim teacher who is awaiting her husband's return
from Mazar-i-Sharif, intersect at a school in Peshawar, Pakistan.
  ISBN 978-0-312-37776-2
  1. Afghan War, 2001—Juvenile fiction. 2. Afghanistan—
History—2001—Juvenile fiction. [1. Afghan War, 2001—
Fiction. 2. Afghanistan—History—2001—Fiction.
3. Refugees—Fiction. 4. Peshawar (Pakistan)—History—
20th century—Fiction.] I. Title.

PZ7.S79346Un 2005
[Fic]—dc22

                                        2004053256

To Wayne, my first best reader and friend

Acknowledgments

Thank you to the following for helping to make a collection of ideas and memories into this book: my writer friends Eleanor McCallie Cooper, Carolyn Moon, Rachel Schulson, Danalise Shavin, Jennie Storey, and Vickie Williams for their sensitive reading of each incarnation of every character and chapter; Mary Montague, who so generously helped me to read the poetry of numbers; Mike Whittle for his help with cricket and things related to the sky; Rachel Parkman for helping me to rejoice in the dance of the stars; Leah Schulson for her astute reading; Beverley Vaughn Hock for her faithful reporting on the seasons of the persimmon tree; Mike Edwards for comparing memories of Afghanistan; Jamshed and Sharaf Tirmizi for helping me to understand more about faith and Islam; Nabila Massoumi for helping me with the Dari language; and Afghan friends met all over the world for sharing their extraordinary stories.

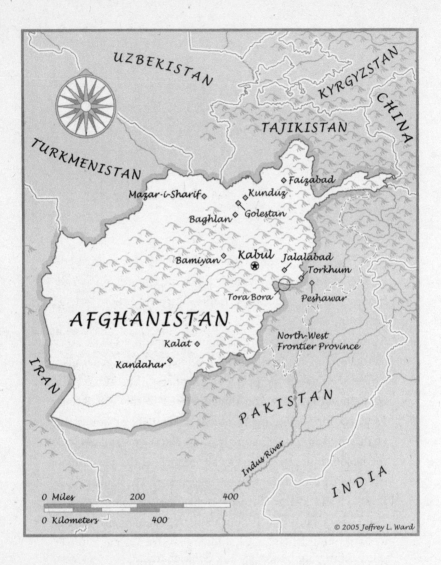

Author's Note

One of the most impoverished nations on earth, Afghanistan is also one of the world's great cultural treasures. It is where the Middle East meets Asia, a rugged nation where mountain ranges, plateaus, ancient trade routes, languages, ethnic groups, and religions have come together over its tumultuous history. Afghanistan's cultural richness is reflected in the variety of faces: the broad, flat visage of the Uzbek, Turkmen, and Kirghiz; the dark, regular-featured majority Pashtun tribesmen; the fair-skinned, amber- and green-eyed Nuristanis, who claim to be descended from Alexander the Great. Afghanistan's languages also reflect this cultural mélange. A Glossary of words that would be used commonly by the mainly Tajik characters of this story appears on page 271. It includes words from Dari (the Afghan dialect of Farsi, or Persian), Urdu (the language of neighboring Pakistan), Arabic (from the Koran), and words rooted in Pashtu and Turkish.

For the purposes of this story, I have taken certain liberties with the timing of some real-life events. The village of Golestan is fictional.

UNDER THE

PERSIMMON TREE

1

The day begins like every day in the Kunduz Hills, following the rhythms of the sun and moon. Before first light—even before the first stars begin to fade—my mother tugs at my quilt.

"Get up, sleepy one," she says. "It's time to light the fire!" I feel as if I've just gone to sleep. How can it be time to begin another day so soon after the last one has ended?

Mada-jan leans then over my older brother, Nur. To him she says, "Get up, sleepy one. It's time to get water so that I can make tea!"

Nur grumbles, and the quilt rustles as he turns

over. But Mada-jan does what she always does when we try to ignore her: she yanks the quilt up from the bottom and tickles his bare feet with a piece of straw. The quilt makes a popping sound as Nur kicks out. But Mada-jan is quick to get out of the way—despite her belly, which is enormous with my unborn brother. I am sure it's a brother because my mother has been well and happy throughout her pregnancy. I have named my unborn brother Habib, which means "beloved friend." I know Habib will be my friend, unlike Nur, who teases me mercilessly.

Before Nur goes out the door, he picks up the nearly empty water tin and flicks a few drops into my face. It's icy and chases away any thought I might have of sleeping a few minutes longer.

"If the rooster is up, so must the hen be up," he says, and his hand sloshes again in the water.

"Nur, stop playing!" Mada-jan says. "Najmah, get up!" She tugs at my quilt again. "After you fetch firewood you must feed this bukri," she says, motioning to the brand-new baby goat that stands on quivering, sticklike legs near the head of the cot where I sleep. She was born yesterday, and her mother won't feed her.

I hold out my hand to the kid, who nuzzles the underside of my fingers, butting my palm with her nose. Then I throw back the quilt and reach for my shawl. The autumn morning air is chilly, and I savor the cool, knowing how hot it will be before noon.

"Baba-jan is already milking the goats, and when he gets back he'll want his breakfast," says Mada-jan, folding my quilt so that I can't change my mind and crawl back under its warmth. At the thought of the milk my father will bring, my stomach grumbles.

Outside, Nur finds the pole and ties the ghee tins to either end of it with goat sinew. He hoists it to his shoulder and waits for me to walk with him to where the path leads down the hill to Baba Darya, the little stream at the bottom. Baba means "old man" as well as "father." We call it "Old Man River" because its thin ribbons twist together like the wisps of an elder's beard.

"I saw a leopard's pug marks in the dust here last night," Nur says, just as we reach the fork in the path that will take me to the woodpile and Nur to the Baba Darya. I hesitate where the two paths split.

"Nur!" Mada-jan says, her voice low with warning. Knowing Nur very well, she has stepped outside the door to listen. "Stop trying to scare her! Najmah, you know there are no leopards here. Now hurry, you two!" Still I hesitate.

"Really!" Nur whispers. "They were this big!" He holds his fist up so I can see it in the creeping light of the sunrise. "It must be a very large leopard."

Then he turns his back and walks, humming, down the hill toward the Baba Darya, the tins bouncing from the ends of the pole across his shoulder.

My heart hammers, and I want to run back to the house, but I know Mada-jan will be angry. I turn and run as fast as I can, all the way to the woodpile. There I spread my shawl on the ground and pile several armloads of wood on top. I feel a tingling along my spine the whole time. I think I see yellow eyes gleaming in the dark to the side of the woodpile. I'm sure I hear a low growl.

"Nur was only teasing," I mutter under my breath. "Nur was only teasing." But I really am convinced a large animal with long, pointed teeth is waiting to pounce on me. I am terribly afraid of leopards, although I have never seen one in my life. Mada-jan reminds me of this every time I complain that Nur has told me he's heard one roar. When the shawl holds as much wood as I can carry, I bind up its corners into a knot and heft the bundle onto my head, then hurry back up the path under the heavy load.

Usually Mada-jan fetches the wood, leaving me to make naan inside our mud-brick house, because she knows I'm afraid. But Habib, who will arrive in just a few days, keeps her off-balance when she walks along the steep, narrow paths. My father worries that she'll tumble down to the bottom of the hill, and so he has asked me to put aside my fear to help my mother. I feel proud that I can do it, even though I am afraid.

I sit outside the curtained front doorway and make a small pyramid of kindling inside the mud oven. Mada-jan brings out the basket that holds the pads of dough she's made and skewers each piece on a hook that she suspends through a hole in the top of the oven. The goat kid butts insistently at my shoulder, wanting to nurse. A few minutes later I hear Nur huffing under the weight of the water as he climbs the last few feet from the Baba Darya.

And only a moment later Baba-jan comes whistling down the path that leads from the pens that hold our sheep and goats at the base of the foothills of the Hindu Kush. He carries a large pail of milk. The light is a pale green behind the snowy mountain peaks that hover over us, and a few morning stars still float there, waiting for the sun to send them on their way.

"We're going to have to take the sheep and goats farther up to feed," Baba-jan says, sitting down cross-legged in one fluid motion. "The hills are parched, and there isn't enough for them to eat." Usually the rains come in spring and summer, and the hills lie curled on themselves, soft and brilliant, like giants sleeping under a green carpet. Now they seem flatter, gray and misty with dust, just as they do in the dead of winter.

But still our farm feeds us. Twice a week Nur and I make many trips carrying the ghee tins up and down the hill to the Baba Darya, which now moves slowly like a baba, too, since there is little water in it. We carry them to the plot where my father grows vegetables and fruit for the market, and flowers for my mother. Baba-jan carefully pours tin after tin of muddy water in a thin stream between the neat rows of apple, apricot, and almond trees.

We shiver in our shawls as we sit on the dark red Turkoman rug outside the curtained front door of our house, eating gruel with goat's milk and bread and sweet green tea. As I eat, I dip my finger into a cup of milk and hold it out for the kid to suck at greedily. The sun rises, and Baba-jan asks Nur to come with him to the plot.

"You can look after the flock yourself, can't you, my little sugar beet?" Baba-jan asks me. His face is scored with lines from working in the hot sun and worrying about the parched crops and grazing lands. I don't want to say that I am afraid to go into the hills by myself, so I nod dumbly. "Good," he says. "Nur can carry water more quickly than you can, and I don't want your mother up in the hills when the baby could come at any time."

I want to tell him that I can carry as much water as Nur, who is not much bigger, and as quickly, too. I am tall, like Mada-jan, and strong like Baba-jan—Nur is thin like Mada-jan and short like Baba-jan. But I bite the inside of my cheek and say nothing.

Mada-jan and I pick up the remains of the food and store it in baskets. We roll up the rug where we sat to eat and bring it inside. Full of milk, the kid curls into a little pile of fur and bone and sleeps just inside the doorway. After we have swept out the house—chickens scattering in a frenzy of angry clucks before our twig brooms—Mada-jan hugs me to her awkwardly, because Habib comes between us.

"You are a good and brave girl," she says, stroking my face. I don't feel brave, but I don't trust my voice to speak, and so I nod as I did to Baba-jan. Mada-jan tucks a sack of dried apricots and small sulaiman raisins and almonds into my pocket, smiling her gratitude even as she nudges me out the door. "I will look after your little bukri for you," she says. "She'll be fat by the time you return."

I lead the sheep and goats up the path to the hills behind the village. Wooden clappers make gentle *thunk*s and *plink*s against the insides of the bronze bells tied around their necks.

We live simply but we have plenty to eat: apples, nuts, apricots, pomegranates, and persimmons from the orchard, vegetables from the garden plot, wheat for bread, eggs, goat's milk—and honey, too. For special occasions Baba-jan slaughters a goat. And the hills are peaceful, although Afghanistan has been at war since Baba-jan was a boy. The mujahideen control the northern part of Afghanistan, and they leave us alone. We give them wheat and vegetables because Baba-jan says they need help to keep the Pashtun talib out of Kunduz.

Usually I spend my days tagging after Nur as we watch the animals graze among the hills. Every year during the hot season, when the sun burns the grass to the roots, we take the flock higher into the hills, so far up that eventually it is too far to come back, and we sleep there under the stars at night. Baba-jan taught us to find al-Qutb, the star that never moves, at the end of the handle of the water ladle. He told us that al-Qutb means "hub," like the hub of a wheel, and the other stars move around it. He knelt by my side and told me to make a fist, and then to point the second knuckle at the star.

"As long as you know the stars, you will never be lost," he said. The Koran says that Allah gave us the stars to be our guides. "Everything depends on the stars. From them you can tell time and distance and you can find your way home." He told us many stories and showed us the shapes of animals and warriors and mythical beasts among the stars. Nur and I retell Baba-jan's star stories over and over again to pass the nights away from home. Baba-jan loves the stars so much that he named me Najmah, which means "star." He also gave Nur his name, which means "light," and we have learned to love the stars as much as Baba-jan loves them.

This is the first time I've gone with the flock alone. Walking up the hill, I am still afraid, but with the sun shining I find it easier to believe there are no leopards in our hills.

From the top of Koh-i-Dil, which overshadows our village of Golestan, people walking along the dirt tracks below look like insects. The donkeys, which carry rocks to repair the road in sack-lined baskets strapped across their backs, look like ants moving in a line.

Although it's been dry for months that never seem to end, the sky holds a promise of rain. Gray clouds have rolled in over the hills to the west, and they dance across the sun. A cool breeze blows. I rest on a large rock, watching the sun and shade play over the sheep and goats, when I hear a rumbling from below. At first I think it's thunder. I walk to the other side of the hill, away from the village, and from there I see a line of pickup trucks—a dozen or more—snaking their way among the rocks and ruts in the dirt tracks far below.

We do not often see automobiles and trucks. The mountain tracks are barely passable, except for camels and donkeys and horses, and people on foot. Our village is very far from a real metaled road such as the one that runs along the Kunduz River.

But everyone recognizes the black Datsun trucks as the vehicles of the Taliban. Everyone is frightened of the Taliban and the heartless Pashtun talib who enforce their rules. We have heard how they lock the people of entire villages inside their houses and burn them to the ground and how they slaughter men like goats, slitting them open and leaving their blood to soak into the ground. There are lists of things that are forbidden by the Taliban: playing music, laughing out loud, keeping a bird to hear its song in the morning, putting pictures of beautiful scenes on the walls, reading books, flying kites. We have heard that women wearing henna on their fingertips have had their fingers chopped off.

The Taliban have said the only thing people can do to enjoy themselves is to walk in the garden and smell the flowers. But ever since the Taliban came to power five years ago, there has been drought. It's as if Allah has banished flowers to punish the Taliban for the evil things they do to people.

I think of running down to warn the people of Golestan, but I'm not certain I can reach the village before the trucks. I turn to see that the sheep and goats are grazing peacefully below me, and decide in an instant. I half run, half tumble down the hill to the village.

When I am within shouting distance, the trucks are within hearing, and Mada-jan stands in front of the purdah draped over the doorway, shaking out laundry and hanging things over the legs of our overturned cots to dry in the sun. Each morning we drag some of the cots outside to make room in the house. The little goat kid nudges against her skirt, looking for more milk. When she hears the trucks, she straightens her back and arranges her blue chadr so that it covers her face against the gaze of the men in the passing vehicles.

"Where is Baba-jan?" I shout, and she extends her arm toward the fields, the opposite direction from where the pickup trucks have come. The vehicles, which are battered and covered with dirt, grind their way through the dust toward our house. Each of them carries three or four men with guns in the back. Mada-jan watches them for a moment before ducking inside.

I change direction and run toward our field below the curve of the hill, calling loudly for Baba-jan. Suddenly I think of another Taliban rule. Men must have beards that you can grab in your fist and still have the hair sticking out at the bottom. Baba-jan has little hair on his face, and although he wears a beard it is not very full or long.

Just seconds after the men in the trucks reach our house, Baba-jan comes running up from the fields, bareheaded except for an embroidered cap. This, too, is against Taliban rules that say all men must wear turbans. The Pashtun talib wear green and brown Army jackets and huge black turbans, and all of them carry guns. The leader holds his rifle against his chest, which is crisscrossed with two leather belts filled with bullets.

Baba-jan turns, extending his arm and laying his hand against Nur's chest to warn him to stay back. Nur resists, pushing his chest against Baba-jan's hand, and his eyes never leave the Pashtun leader. Baba-jan takes me by the shoulders then and turns me toward our house, giving me a gentle shove.

"Take care of your mother," he says. I don't grasp what his words mean, but I'm used to obeying, so I duck inside the purdah, where Mada-jan crouches, looking through the crack between the woven hanging and the doorframe. I join her, bending forward to peer over her head as Baba-jan greets the men in the trucks.

"Ah-salaam-aleikum," Baba-jan says, not giving the traditional friendly greeting, "mande nabash"—may you never be tired. The Pashtun talib leader ignores the slight and looks past Baba-jan at Nur.

"So your son wants to fight?" he says with a slow little grin. He doesn't return Baba-jan's greeting. Mada-jan sucks her breath in through her teeth.

"He's just a boy," Baba-jan says, standing between the man and Nur and holding his hands out to his sides with his palms open in a silent appeal. The Pashtun continues to stare at my brother and does not look at Baba-jan. His rudeness frightens me, for such behavior is an insult that cannot be ignored. This man has a gun, which Baba-jan does not. Then the man turns his back on Baba-jan, an even worse insult. But Baba-jan does not react. The Pashtun speaks to one of his men in Pashtu. The men spread out and Baba-jan turns to watch them.

"We want wheat and chickens and sugar," the leader says.

"I can give you some," Baba-jan answers. "But we have little since the drought . . ." This is true and

I hold my breath. I am afraid the talib leader will shoot him if we don't give them food.

"You had enough to give our enemies," says the talib leader, waving his gun in a menacing way. "You will give us more than you gave to them." Baba-jan does not reply. He no longer looks at the leader, but watches the other men, who are already searching for food.

Some of the men carry woven bags filled with wheat and sugar from the lean-to at the back of our house. Mada-jan and I hear the metallic *twang* of the ghee tin as they lift it, still full of cooking oil, from the ground. We hear the clayey *thunk* of wooden lids as they're lifted from the tops of the earthenware jars where we keep salt and tea. We hear men curse and grunt as they dive for chickens that squawk and flap their wings to escape. I crouch and lean against Mada-jan, who puts her hand out through the curtain to gesture to Baba-jan. She makes little sounds in her throat as she tries to get his attention. She doesn't want him to resist because she's afraid they'll hurt him—they might even kill him.

Then the purdah is whisked aside, and one of the black-turbaned Pashtun sticks his head inside. Mada-jan and I huddle together, and Mada-jan draws me underneath her chadr. But I see what the man does:

he grabs up the little bukri and sticks it under his arm.

"No!" I shout, and Mada-jan holds me against her, keeping me from running after him. The bukri cries out in a bleating that sounds like a human baby, and I want to snatch her away from this human leopard.

When the men have gathered the food we have stored in the baskets, sacks, and earthen jars in the lean-to, the leader turns and says to Baba-jan, "To repay us for having helped our enemy, you must come and fight with the Taliban."

"No!" Mada-jan cries. She shoves aside the curtain and stands to run to Baba-jan, who turns toward her and holds up his hand, as if to say, "Stop!" He looks at her for a long moment.

"It will be all right," he says to her. This time it's my turn to hold on to Mada-jan with all my strength as she struggles to run to him.

"I will go," Baba-jan says, turning back to face the Pashtun talib without raising his voice.

"Your son, too," says the man. "He wants to fight, and we wouldn't want to disappoint him."

"He's just a boy," Baba-jan says again, and the man raises the butt of his rifle as if to strike Baba-jan in the face.

Baba-jan ducks and turns, and the blow hits his shoulder. He looks at Mada-jan for several seconds. Tears stream down her face, and she repeats over and over again, "You can't go. Please! What will become of us?"

"Whatever happens, stay here," Baba-jan says to her as they grab him and Nur roughly by the arms.

"Bring your guns," the leader says.

"I will come back," Baba-jan says, looking back over his shoulder at Mada-jan as they begin to drag Nur away. "Do you hear? Don't leave, no matter what!" The leader shoves Baba-jan so that he almost falls, and tells him to be quiet.

"Your guns!" the leader repeats and hammers Baba-jan's shoulder with the heel of his hand, knocking him off balance again.

"I have no guns," Baba-jan says, looking at the man directly. The Pashtun talib mutters something, and the men shove and drag Baba-jan and my brother toward the Datsun pickup trucks.

Again Mada-jan tries to go to him, but I grab her by the arm. "We cannot stop them," I whisper. "They might hurt Baba-jan and Nur if we resist." I hold on to her with all my strength, and she throws back her head and wails.

I hear the pickup trucks leave, but I am struggling with Mada-jan and cannot see them. I lead her to the cot in the corner of the room and pull her down onto it. She continues to wail, but her body goes limp, which frightens me more than if she were to go on struggling. She curls onto her side like an infant, and tucks her head under her wrists and remains that way.

I go to the door and push aside the purdah. All I can see is the dust that billows in round brownish clouds as the trucks lumber away, dodging the holes in the dirt track.

2

Nusrat steps down from the motorized cycle rickshaw at the end of a dusty, narrow alley behind a row of houses in University Town, an affluent section of Peshawar. She steps lightly around a gray-striped cat that lies in a tiny patch of sunlight trying to ignore the three kittens that pounce on her bent tail. A child with bare feet and wearing a red flowered dress dashes from a courtyard and scoops the kittens up in her arms. The cat scampers after the child as she disappears again behind the painted blue metal gate.

Nusrat draws her burqa forward to adjust the

crocheted rectangle in front of her eyes so she can see to avoid goat droppings and garbage that lie in her way. Gray water from the baths and kitchens of wealthy families sloshes over the edges of the concrete-lined open sewers that flow on either side of the footpath.

In the cool autumn air, Nusrat forgets how suffocating the folds of the burqa's synthetic fabric can be in hot weather, and how peering through the crocheted latticework eyepiece can feel like looking through the bars of a prison. The traditional head covering has come to feel almost normal to Nusrat, whose blond hair and blue eyes drew stares when she went to the bazaar without it when she was new to this conservative capital of Pakistan's North-West Frontier.

Her name, too, has come to seem like her real, her only name. Her very American parents in Watertown, New York, had named her Elaine when she was born, a name she'd never really felt had much to do with her.

When Nusrat reaches the elaborately filigreed wrought iron and steel gate that opens onto the back courtyard of the house at the end of the alley, she shifts the basket of persimmons she carries to her other hand and rings the bell. A round disk swivels back from a two-inch hole, where a dark eye appears.

A black fringe of lashes flutters across the eye, and bolts slide back into the locks on the other side.

"Ah-salaam-aleikum!" says the Pashtun gate-keeper as he swings the gate open. The golden, sunlit courtyard and the well-tended potted plants and trees inside are a surprising contrast to the dark passage-way where Nusrat stands just outside the gate.

Once inside, Nusrat pushes her burqa back over her head, and her sister-in-law, Asma, gathers it up to keep it from falling onto the ground. Asma greets her with a kiss on each cheek and a warm hug. She throws Nusrat's burqa over her arm and takes the basket of persimmons.

"Wow!" says Asma. "You have new jeans."

"My mother sent them from the States," says Nusrat. "She says she'll send you a pair if I let her know your size. I wrote back immediately and told her you wear an eight. That's right, isn't it?"

"It's been so long since I've worn American clothes," Asma says. "You are the *best* sister! I'm sure a size eight will fit." Nusrat smiles, but a little tug in the vicinity of her heart reminds her of her real sister, Margaret, who died when Nusrat was ten. Asma reaches out to touch Nusrat's hair. Then she looks nervously over her shoulder. The guard at the gate is a Pashtun. And so are the gardener and the laundry-man. The family don't talk much out in the courtyard because they're never sure the Pashtu-speaking Taliban won't pressure the servants to talk. Nusrat and Asma shift self-consciously into their more formal "courtyard" behavior toward each other.

"I've missed your sunlight," says Asma, tucking a stray lock of Nusrat's hair behind her ear. The gesture reminds Nusrat of her mother. It had annoyed her as a child to have her mother arrange and re-arrange her hair, and yet she loves it when her sister-in-law does it. The thought brings unexpected tears to the backs of Nusrat's eyes. She hasn't seen her mother in seven months, since the day she and Faiz left New York to live in Peshawar, just thirty miles from Pakistan's border with Afghanistan. She seldom thinks of her mother, but she thinks of Margaret almost every day.

"And I have missed yours," Nusrat responds, smiling fondly at her husband's younger sister. Just then Jamshed, Asma's ten-year-old son, runs from a doorway and takes his aunt by the hand, tossing questions and comments at her faster than she can catch them.

"Auntie, Auntie!" he shouts, pulling her toward the edge of the courtyard, where cane seats are arranged around a table that's set for tea. "Where have you been? I've missed you *so* much! Have you heard? They're fighting in Kunduz—Father says dozens of people have been killed!" He pulls at Nusrat until his mother makes him stop. "They're putting out the eyes of the shepherds who won't give them food, and—"

"Jamshed!" says his mother sharply. "That's enough." Nusrat feels light-headed at Jamshed's news, and Asma directs her to sit in one of the cane chairs. Jamshed gallops over to the settee beside Nusrat's chair and bounces up and down on the hard edge of its seat.

"Don't upset your auntie," Asma says, and Jamshed fidgets, twisting a piece of cane that's come loose from the seat while Asma goes to arrange for the tea to be brought.

"How's your cricket team doing?" Nusrat asks him. "What position do you play?"

"This year I'm the wicket keeper," Jamshed says, brightening again. "I stumped two players last match. But our team isn't doing so well. We've been beaten twice by Acheson—and we won every match against them last season." Elaine has worked hard to understand cricket, which is incomprehensible to most Americans. Jamshed knows her interest is entirely for his sake. He looks down at the open toes of his shoes. "Auntie," he says, "when will Uncle Faiz be home?"

Nusrat leans forward and smiles at her husband's nephew. "I wish I knew, bacha," she says, her throat tightening around the words. She wishes desperately that she could say "Next week," or "In a month." But Faiz left four months before, not knowing when he'd return, and they have not heard from him at all in the last three weeks. At first Nusrat felt certain that Allah would protect Faiz. He had gone to an area north of Kandahar on the road to Kalat to establish a free clinic.

But just a month earlier the Twin Towers fell in New York, and Nusrat knew the world had changed, that no one was safe. She began to worry about Faiz with every day that passed with no word from him. When the American President announced the United States would bomb Afghanistan, Nusrat felt her heart begin to break into fragments. And now she lives every day with dread.

Maha, the elderly maid, brings a tray heavily loaded with a cozy-covered teapot, small plates, meat patties, and biscuits. Nusrat stands to help her, and the bent ayah smiles a loose-toothed smile before setting the tray down on the table. She straightens and takes Nusrat's arm in both of her hands, which are crooked with arthritis, and holds it tightly while she questions her.

"Are you keeping well?" asks Maha, searching Nusrat's face with her milky eyes as if looking for a sign of health. "Are you eating enough?" Maha was

Asma and Faiz's ayah when they were children, and they both love her like a grandmother. She still treats them and their spouses as if they're too young to look after themselves.

"Yes, yes, Maha," Nusrat replies, gently patting one of the hands that hold on to her arm with surprising strength. "I am well—just missing my husband." Maha clucks her tongue and says, "Masha' Allah, God's will." She squeezes Nusrat's hand before turning back to the kitchen. Asma chuckles and leans forward.

"What she really wants to know is whether you're pregnant," Asma whispers, and Nusrat smiles.

"I wish now that I were," Nusrat says. They drink their tea and talk of household and family news. Jamshed slouches down in his seat and swings his feet back and forth while he listens. When they have finished their tea, Asma stands and Nusrat and Jamshed follow her into the house, through the purplish haze cast by the single fluorescent tube in the hallway that leads to a large sitting room on one side and a formal dining room on the other before coming to the kitchen at the back of the house.

Before Faiz left, he tried to persuade Nusrat to live with his mother and sister and their family in this large, comfortable house in a pleasant section of the city. But Nusrat insisted that she must have her own house near the refugee camps so she could keep open her school for Afghan children who have been torn from their homes and farms and flocks.

"If you're going to help people, I can't just sit at home and drink tea," she said. Faiz agreed only because he knew how determined she was.

"Thanks for the persimmons," says Asma. "I'll use them for a pudding for tonight." She pushes back the curtain that covers the doorway to the kitchen and holds it aside for Jamshed and Nusrat.

"They're all I have to bring," says Nusrat. "I keep the other fruits and vegetables from the garden for my students. Their mothers come back from the bazaar empty-handed nearly every day now."

"Jamshed, go do your schoolwork," Asma says, and Jamshed's face falls.

"Mada-jan," he says, wheedling, beseeching her with his eyes. "I want to hear news of Uncle Faiz . . ."

"Can't he stay?" Nusrat asks. "Faiz is his favorite uncle and Jamshed is our only nephew." Asma looks a little startled. It's not like Nusrat to interfere in matters regarding Asma's son. Reluctantly she agrees, and Jamshed rushes to get a chair to place next to the doorway before his mother can change her mind.

Asma gestures for Nusrat to sit on a stool beside her while she resumes kneading bread dough in a large shallow wooden bowl. "Have you heard they've closed the clinic in Kalat?" Asma asks, turning up the volume on the CD player in the window well. Its sound covers their conversation in case any of the servants should try to listen.

"No!" says Nusrat. "Why?" Asma shakes her head.

"I have no idea. Faiz ordered it closed himself. I heard this yesterday from Babar, who said he saw Faiz give one of the men a note to carry with him to Peshawar. That was about two weeks ago. Babar thought perhaps it was for you . . ." Babar is the son of a neighbor who had gone to help Faiz set up his clinic. He has come home again to take care of his sick father.

"You know I'd let you know immediately if I had a note from him!" says Nusrat. "It's been too long since we've heard anything. I don't like it, Asma. I wonder why he didn't give the note to Babar . . ." She hasn't intended for the intensity of her fear to show through her voice, but there it is, blooming like a lurid flower. Asma looks across her shoulder at Nusrat and says nothing for a while.

"I know why, sister," says Asma then, pushing her hair back from her forehead with a flour-dusted wrist. "Babar didn't receive word of his father's illness until after Faiz had left for Mazar-i-Sharif. Perhaps he will open another clinic there. Perhaps they expect the fighting to be heavy in the North."

"I feel better knowing Faiz gave someone a note to deliver to us," says Nusrat. "He knows we all worry about him. It isn't like him to let us worry."

"It's quite possible something happened to the one who carried the message," says Asma. "Perhaps it's a good thing Babar didn't carry it."

"Perhaps the messenger was delayed and will come soon," adds Nusrat brightly. She looks over at Jamshed, who has been listening intently, his eyes round. She holds out her arms to him, and he comes to her and lets her pull him onto her lap.

3

My mother cries for most of the two days after the Taliban took Baba-jan and my brother away. She lies on her side, curled up on the cot, and stares at the insides of her wrists as if they hold some secret map that will tell her where she might find them. Her tears pool in the well at the inner corner of her eye, then roll down over her nose and drop onto the quilt beneath her. She doesn't eat, or sleep, or talk, or wipe the tears away. She seems to barely breathe. Once or twice a day she holds out her hand for me to help her to her feet so she can use the small porcelain pot I have put under her bed.

The afternoon of that terrible first day I recognize the voice of our neighbor Bibi Usmani at our door. "Is anyone there?" she calls out. Bibi Usmani gave cuttings of many kinds of flowers from her own garden to Baba-jan so that he could grow them for my mother. I pull a shawl up over my mother and go out to greet Bibi Usmani.

"Mande nabash, may you never be tired," I say, and she nods. She makes a soft clicking sound with her tongue.

"Jor bash, may you be well," she says, greeting me in return.

"We're leaving for Torkhum in three days—all of us. The village men have all been taken—including boys too young to fight. The rest of us are going to cross the border at Torkhum and wait in the refugee camps in Peshawar," she says. She stands alone, her hand resting on a walking stick. Bibi Usmani has a bad leg, and I wonder if she means to walk all the way to Peshawar, which would be a very long walk of many days for someone with two good legs.

"The baby could come at any time," I say. "We cannot leave."

"All the men have gone," says Bibi Usmani. "The Taliban have taken all of the food, and it isn't safe to stay. We will wait for our men in Peshawar." In times of war many Afghans go to Peshawar in

Pakistan when it isn't safe to stay on the land. My family has never gone to Peshawar.

Just then the crown of a striped gray turban appears at the rim of the hill as someone trudges up the steep path toward the house. Bibi Usmani draws her chadr across her face just as Uncle Mohiuddin, Baba-jan's brother, appears at the top of the path.

Bibi Usmani greets him, and he grunts in response. Then she turns to me.

"Come to my house if you need me," she says. "We won't leave for three days." I thank her, and she brushes past my uncle on the path with a brief greeting, and then disappears over the edge of the hill that descends to the village.

Uncle is a big man, heavyset and awkward, not muscular and compact like Baba-jan. And unlike Baba-jan, who has a ready smile and an irrepressible laugh, Uncle wears a scowl on his heavy brow.

"Where is your mother?" he asks.

"She isn't well. Her time is near." Uncle moves forward, as if to enter the house, but I step into the space between him and the doorway to keep him from going inside. He reaches his hand out, as if to draw the purdah aside.

"You can't go in," I say. My heart is hammering. One part of my mind is afraid Baba-jan might be angry with me for being disrespectful toward his brother. But I have a strong sense that he wouldn't want Uncle to go into our house either.

Uncle and Baba-jan grew up the only sons in a family of many daughters. Uncle left when Grandfather needed his help on their farm. He never said goodbye or where he was going, and he returned only to claim his part of the land after Grandfather's death. Baba-jan said Uncle had broken Grandmother's heart. She died just a year after he went away.

Although Uncle's land adjoins ours, we never see him. He and Baba-jan argue because Uncle grows poppies in his fields. Baba-jan says opium is a bad thing, and he tries to persuade Uncle to grow food instead. Uncle laughs and says he'd rather have money than turnips.

"Everyone in the village is leaving," Uncle says, looking up at Koh-i-Dil and the Hindu Kush Range, which stretches out in layer after purple layer behind our mountain. "You and your mother should do the same." Koh-i-Dil means "Heart Mountain," and when one has lived from infancy in such a place it tears at the heart to leave it.

"My mother and I will stay," I say. My uncle laughs, and his large stomach wobbles under his tunic.

"The Taliban are preparing for a great war

against the Americans," he says. "They've taken away the men and all of the food. You can't stay with nothing to eat."

"If you can stay, we can stay," I say. I wonder why my uncle hasn't been forced to go with the Taliban. Suddenly I realize what Baba-jan meant when he told my mother to stay here until he comes back. He worries that Uncle will steal our land. Perhaps he is more worried about Uncle than he is about the Taliban.

"Many have already gone to Pakistan," Uncle says, gesturing toward the lip of the hill, where Bibi Usmani had disappeared just moments before. "It would be much safer for you to go with them. There you would have food and you'd be safe from bombs and fighting. You'd best go before they close the border."

"We will be safe enough here," I say. "We must look after the land and—" I stop myself from saying the animals. Who knows whether they're safe from Uncle?

"I can look after your father's land," Uncle says, narrowing his eyes. My mother cries out then, and I go to her, leaving Uncle standing outside the doorway.

I think perhaps her labor has begun. I pick up a pan of water and wash her face, but she closes her eyes and goes to sleep. A little later I hear Uncle's footsteps as he walks around to the back of the house. I think perhaps he is searching for the sheep and goats. I've left them in the meadow on the side of Koh-i-Dil, about an hour's walk away. I hear quiet rustling as Uncle lifts the lids to the empty storage jars and baskets at the back of the house and then his footsteps as he walks away toward the path that leads down the hill.

I never leave my mother's side over the next day, except to carry water from the Baba Darya to the animals, who graze on the hillside above the house, where there is little water. I eat apples that were inside the house when the Taliban came. They had escaped their notice, as had the stale bread left in the basket the morning Baba-jan and Nur went away.

The morning of the following day Bibi Usmani looks in on us again. Habib has not yet made his appearance. I leave my mother sleeping and go out when I hear her hoarse voice outside the door.

"You cannot stay here," Bibi Usmani says. "Everyone says the bombing could begin at any moment. And there are rumors the Pakistanis will soon close the border." Her brow is furrowed. She and her children each carry a stick and a cloth bag of food. Their donkey is piled high with cooking pots, quilts, baskets, earthen jars, and rugs. Lashed to the top of the pile like a precarious crown is a large brass samovar. It's clear they are leaving.

"My mother cannot travel," I say, trying to be brave. But my voice quavers. "We must stay for at least the next few days, until the baby comes. Then perhaps . . ."

Bibi Usmani takes my hand and presses a small brown paper packet into my palm. "Give her this in some warm milk," she says. "It will prevent too much bleeding. My brother Akhtar and his family will come soon from Badakhshan. I've asked them to stop here. Akhtar fought with the mujahideen against the Soviets. He knows the hills and the safest way to travel. Perhaps you can come with him and his family." I thank her and manage not to cry. We stand looking at each other for a moment, and I wonder whether I will ever see her again. It occurs to me that she thinks the same thought as she strokes my cheek and says goodbye. Then they are gone.

I go back inside and beg my mother to eat, but she won't even take water, and I am becoming afraid she and the unborn Habib will die. And I will be left all alone.

I try not to think about Bibi Usmani and the other villagers walking to Pakistan, but I am afraid to be left here, with only Uncle Mohiuddin to stand between us and the Taliban. He would rather see us dead so he can take our land and our flocks, I think bitterly.

I begin to feel hopeless. I can't imagine surviving without Baba-jan and Nur to look after the animals and tend the fields. We all four work from before the sun rises until we go to sleep every day, and that is how we stay alive. The Taliban have already taken the chickens. I am terrified they'll come back and take the sheep and goats, what fruit and vegetables still ripen in the field, and our house and leave us to starve to death on the side of the mountain.

I have forgotten my childish quarrels with Nur— I am no longer angry with him for scaring me about the leopard, and for saying I can't carry water as far as he can. It's as if these things never happened, and all I want is to see the top of his head and Baba-jan's as they trudge up the hill, carrying water from the Baba Darya.

I awaken the morning of the next day and decide I have to do something or we surely will die, even if the Taliban do not come back. I don't want to leave my mother alone with her time so near, but I have no choice. I arise long before first light. Mada-jan still lies silently on her cot, staring and weeping.

I do not even think of leopards as I go to the woodpile and return carrying several days' worth of wood. I go to the Baba Darya and carry the same load that Nur always carries—two ghee tins filled to the top with water—without spilling a drop. The whole time I think about what I will say to my mother.

I gather together the meager supplies the Taliban missed inside the house. I go to Baba-jan's field and pick the few half-formed squash and misshapen eggplants that remain. I dig and find some potatoes and an onion. I brew tea and make naan and roast potatoes with onion, and cut the vegetables for a spicy stew. I beg my mother to eat. When she still refuses I say to her, "You may choose not to live, but the baby and I need you. And the flock needs food. I don't want to die."

Her eyes flicker, and she looks at me as if it's the first time she's seen me in three days. After a moment she holds out her hand for me to help her up, and she sits stiffly. Her lips seem sealed shut, and I bring her a cup of water. When she has drunk it, she hands me the empty cup and places her hands on her belly and straightens her back.

"I must get up," she says hoarsely. I help her to stand, and slowly she walks to the door and goes outside into the sunlight. When she comes back she sits again, and I give her a bowl of potatoes and some tea.

"I'm going up to the high pastures to cut grass for the animals," I say. She nods. "Are you well enough to stay by yourself for a day?" She nods again.

"Go," she says. "Today the baby will come." I hesitate.

"I should stay, then."

"I will be fine." She waves her hand toward the door for me to go. "You're right. The animals will need food and water. This baby will come without trouble."

I am not sure what to do, and to fill the time while I think, I climb the hill and bring the herd back down, and lock the animals in their pens.

When I come back, Mada-jan is sweeping the house. She has rolled up the carpets, and outside the doorway a mound of fresh straw waits to be spread over the dirt floor.

"Najmah," says Mada-jan, "you can see that I am fine. You must go. When you come back, you will have a new brother."

Still I hesitate. I wish Bibi Usmani still lived down beside the Baba Darya, and that she would come to stay until Habib is safely in my mother's arms. But she does not, and no amount of wishing will make it so. Reluctantly I give my mother the packet of powder and tell her Bibi Usmani's instructions for taking it, then kiss her goodbye.

I climb to the high grazing ground and cut grass,

carrying it back to the goats and sheep. The next afternoon, after I have delivered a third load of cut fodder to the animals, I hurry down the hill to check on my mother. I find her sitting on a cot inside the house, holding Habib, who is wrapped in a shawl and wailing inconsolably. She smiles down at him and hands him to me when I sit beside her.

"His birth was more difficult for him than it was for me," she says as she lays her arm across my shoulders. I touch his perfect pink cheek, and he turns his mouth toward my finger. "He's hungry," says my mother. She unbuttons her tunic and feeds him. Within a few seconds he is sound asleep.

Habib's skin is not mottled, as most newborns' skin is. He takes a deep breath and lies quietly, each of his features perfectly formed. Perhaps the complete rest my mother has had for the days before his birth was good for him.

"You hold him while I bathe," says my mother, taking up the washbasin to fill it with water.

"You should rest," I say. She waves her hand at me and goes out to the water pot. After she has bathed and dressed in a bright flowered daman and combed her hair, she puts the clothing she was wearing into a basket to be laundered and then torn up for rags.

We put the sleeping Habib on the cot with rolled

quilts on either side of him. I sweep the wet straw and blood from the floor and bury it with the afterbirth a short distance from the house, just over the edge of the hill, but not too close to the path down to the village. When I come back from beating the carpets, I stand beside the doorway. My mother has pulled the purdah back to let the late afternoon breeze clear the smell of blood and wet straw from the room. I watch as she lies on the cot beside Habib, whispering prayers into his tiny ear. For the first time in four days I forget my fear and feel happy.

"Allah will forgive us if we do not follow the traditions now," she says, smiling slightly. "We have all we can do to stay alive. When your father and Nur come home, we will perform the ceremonies and celebrate Habib's birth properly."

Once again I believe the sun will continue to rise in the morning and the water will continue to flow in the Baba Darya.

My mother builds a fire, leaving me to sit with Habib. I am tired from hard work and from fear. I am relieved that Habib has been born healthy and that my mother has decided to live. Before I finish eating, I am overcome with a desire to sleep and uncertainty about what lies ahead.

"Your father will return," my mother says, crouching in front of me on the Turkoman carpet beside the front door of our house. She smooths my hair with both hands. "We will be here when he comes, just as he asked."

I fall asleep without realizing I have gone inside the house or lain down or closed my eyes. I don't awaken until the sun rises high above Koh-i-Dil.

NUSRAT
Peshawar, Pakistan

4

Nusrat stops looking for the postman at the metal gate outside her small, slightly decrepit bungalow on Jehangir Road near the international bazaar. But she can't help hearing the jingle of his bicycle bell along the unnamed rutted lane that runs beside the garden wall. She asks her servant, Husna, to check the mailbox every afternoon when she hears its lid close, and scolds herself for being too quick to hear, too disappointed when Husna brings in the handful of bills, flyers from rug merchants, restaurants, and carpenters.

Occasionally Husna brings a letter from Nusrat's

mother addressed to "Mrs. Elaine Perrin Faiz," and Nusrat reads it carefully. When she and Faiz first came to Peshawar, her mother wrote to say how heartbroken she and Nusrat's father were that she had become a Muslim and moved so far away. Nusrat writes around these comments in her return letters, telling her parents only about her visits with Jamshed and Asma and Faiz's mother, how they've made her a part of the family, and the stories her students tell about their lives as shepherds, or about the colors and smells in the bazaars.

Gradually references to "your betrayal" stop, and Nusrat's mother writes only of things that happen in Watertown: who marries, who falls ill, and who has gone on a trip to visit relatives in the Midwest. Nusrat feels more relaxed about her mother, and her mind's eye remembers the bland surroundings in which she grew up almost with affection. Sometimes she even thinks about going home for a visit.

But there is no letter from Faiz. He's too busy running a clinic in Mazar-i-Sharif, she tells herself. The fighting is heavy there and American jets have begun to drop bombs. She must remember the people in Mazar-i-Sharif and how he helps them. She must do something to keep from worrying. A party, she decides, a party to celebrate—what? What is there to celebrate when Faiz is in danger and she hasn't heard anything from him in more than a month? What, possibly??? She chides herself for thinking this way.

The electricity is off most evenings after nine o'clock, and those nights she brushes her hair in her nightgown by the glow of a kerosene lantern. On one such evening she remembers sleeping with her sister in the lake cottage that had no bedroom doors. In the living room their parents talked softly by the light of a kerosene lamp. Elaine and Margaret had gone to bed with the flashlight from their father's toolbox hidden under the pillow. When the lamp was blown out and their parents went to bed, they made a tent by tucking a blanket around the top of the window screen and anchoring the bottom under the mattress.

They pushed their pillows and the other blanket together to make furniture for their tent and lay with their flannel-clad legs twined together, reading *Black Beauty* by the flashlight until Margaret fell asleep.

Nusrat thinks of another night when she and Margaret sat out in the top field of their grandfather's farm near Watertown, New York, the air sweet with the scent of freshly mown hay. Margaret had Grandpa's rickety old brass telescope trained on the sky looking for meteors that streaked past faster than she could find them with the long barrel of the scope. "There goes another one!" said Elaine, but Margaret would not give up on finding one with the telescope.

Suddenly Nusrat thinks of the meteor shower that lights up the northern sky each November. She's not even contemplating an event to celebrate when it comes to her. Her favorite heavenly event is a clear, cold November night sky filled with thousands of shooting stars. Faiz will be under those same stars. How can she not celebrate them?

On her visit to her in-laws the next day she waits until they are assembled at the dinner table: her mother-in-law, Fatima; Asma; Jamshed; Asma's husband, Sultan; and Nusrat. She announces that she will have dinner at her house the following week so they can see the display of shahab, or shooting stars, together.

Fatima, a birdlike woman with short-cropped, snow-white hair, bright dark eyes, and quick movements, smiles fondly at her daughter-in-law. "Good, good, Nusrat," she says. "Faiz would be proud of you for carrying on." Fatima was an English professor at the University of Kabul until the family fled from the Taliban to Pakistan, where they have been waiting for the government in Afghanistan to change again. She speaks in clipped British English that is perfect in syntax and pronunciation, words that sound so fatalistic to Nusrat that they cause a dull thump in her chest.

"Meteors?" Asma asks, not attempting to conceal the skepticism in her voice. "Why do you want to stay up until the wee hours in the cold to see meteors?"

"Because they're very beautiful," says Nusrat. "And this year they'll be especially bright—the weather is forecast to be clear and not too cold. It will be a lovely night."

"It's a natural spectacle, Asma!" Sultan chimes in supportively. "I've seen them here and in America last year, and it was deeply moving. You won't be sorry, darling." Sultan is a tall, muscular man with broad shoulders, a clean-shaven face, and a shining, bald head. He was chair of the department of education at the University of Kabul in what the family refers to as "back before . . . ," letting the end of the phrase trail off. What they mean is "back before the Taliban began its reign of terror under the fundamentalist government in 1996."

"Capital idea, Nusrat! Shall I bring some music?"

"That would be wonderful, Sultan," says Nusrat gratefully. Sultan has tape-recorded folk music from all parts of Afghanistan. He has an extensive collection of Persian, Turkman, and tribal music with flutes, drums, bagpipes, stringed instruments, and vocalists that Nusrat loves. Sultan is a gentle soul with the heart of a poet, much like Faiz in that way, she thinks, and her heart twists gently at the thought of her husband.

"What's a meteorite?" asks Jamshed, who is immediately enthralled with everything Nusrat suggests.

"I'll bet you can find tons about meteorites and comets on the Internet," Sultan says to Jamshed.

"But I want to hear what Auntie-jan knows about meteorites," Jamshed says.

"I'll tell you just a little," says Nusrat. "Then you can tell me what you find on the Internet. Okay?" Jamshed nods his head enthusiastically.

"Meteorites are bits of rock that fall from frozen comets when they pass by the sun. The ice melts, leaving clouds of dust and water and pebbles in the comet's wake. When the earth comes along in its orbit around the sun, it passes through this cloud, and some of the particles enter Earth's atmosphere. They burn up before they fall to the ground, and they make bright arcs in the sky as they burn and fall."

"Never mind the meteors," Fatima says. "What will you have for dinner?" As Maha clears the table, Jamshed and Sultan go off to look up meteorites on the Internet before the electricity goes off for the night. The women sit for a while drinking jasmine-scented green tea and talking about food—recipes and what's available in the bazaar.

"You won't find many people watching meteorites here, Nusrat," Fatima says. "In this part of the world people believe everything is an omen. They call shooting stars 'swords,' and they believe seeing one means that you will soon breathe your last allotted breath in this lifetime. So nobody wants to see meteorites."

"But everyone in this family is well educated," Nusrat says. "Surely you don't believe that!"

"Not believe," says Fatima, "but when I was a child my mother kept us in at night so we wouldn't see shahab and she told us this myth about things in the sky. I know it's silly, but I can't help having this feeling about it."

"Is that why you're not interested?" Nusrat asks, turning to Asma, who shrugs and changes the subject. But in the end they agree to come to Nusrat's for dinner, and afterward to lie against bolsters in the garden and watch the sky full of ice and rock dust.

Several days before the party Nusrat and Husna busily prepare the house and garden, which form a compound with a small servant's quarters and kitchen jutting out at the back, and a veranda with a clothesline from which sheets flap in the unconvincing pale sunlight. At the corner of the garden near the crossing of Jehangir Road and the unnamed lane, Nusrat lovingly tends a plot where in the summer she grows herbs and a few vegetables: tomatoes, crescent-shaped eggplants, peppers, and beans. Her winter crop of squash and spinach, broccoli and cabbage is almost ready to harvest.

A large persimmon tree stands in the center of the dusty yard behind the house. In spring, summer, and early fall its canopy covers nearly half of the space enclosed within the stucco wall that surrounds the entire compound. Under this tree Nusrat conducts her Persimmon Tree School, founded to teach the children of the Shahnawaz refugee camp. The week of the party, after the children leave each afternoon, Nusrat and Husna get busy with preparations.

The powerfully sweet scent of the persimmon tree hangs in the air. The leaves are gone, but many persimmons still ripen on the empty branches, reminding Nusrat of her grandfather's Christmas pear tree, which kept its fruit until snow fell. A bitter edge cuts into the sweetness of the scent, just as it does in the taste of the fruit. Nusrat has tried to describe persimmons in letters to her parents, but finally she decided it was indescribable for anyone who hasn't tasted the fruit.

Husna, a small woman wearing a widow's white shalwar kameez, her graying dark hair tied back in a bun, sweeps the last leaves into a pile and puts them in the mulch bin for the garden. They clean the house top to bottom. They spend the day of the dinner washing rice, pounding spices, shelling almonds and pistachio nuts, marinating lamb in coriander and ginger and yogurt, and boiling the milk, rice, green cardamom, almonds, and honey for kheer, Fatima's favorite dessert. They arrange bolsters and woven cushions around the beautiful dark red-and-blue Oushak carpet that Fatima gave Faiz and Nusrat as a wedding gift. Nusrat places oil lamps and vases of mums around the courtyard.

When the bell rings at the gate that evening Nusrat is ready. Her skin is scented from the ginger blossoms from India that she put in her bathwater. She wears a fresh tunic and a skirt that has small mirrors embroidered into it with gold thread. Her yellow hair is twisted into a knot at the back of her head. She and Husna greet her guests at the gate, and Fatima holds on to Nusrat for a long time. When Nusrat steps back, tears brim in Fatima's eyes. Nusrat knows she is thinking of Faiz and her own husband, who was killed when his automobile hit a land mine in a Kabul street early in the Soviet war in 1980.

The day has been warm for November, and they sit in the courtyard around the Oushak to eat in the light of the lanterns. Husna and Nusrat serve the food kneeling over the beautiful old flowered carpet, passing the steaming hot naan in a linen-covered basket.

After the dishes and remnants of the meal are cleared, Husna brings more bolsters and cushions and sweet green tea flavored with cardamom, and a whiskey for Sultan.

"Will that be all, memsaheb?" Husna asks Nusrat.

"Aren't you staying to watch the shahab?" Nusrat asks. She's been talking about the meteorites with Husna for more than a week. Husna shakes her head and wishes everyone a good night before hurrying off to her room behind the kitchen. Nobody comments, but Nusrat knows Husna thinks of the meteorites in terms of omen.

They sit wrapped in light woolen shawls against the chilling night air and listen to the music, waiting for the sky to dance with the detritus of comets. Asma gathers her shawl around her. "It's too cold out here," she says. "I'm going inside."

"Asma, please stay," says Nusrat. "I'll bring you a quilt." But Asma hurries inside. Shortly afterward Fatima joins her. Jamshed falls asleep, and only Sultan and Nusrat are left when the first meteorite slings its icy arc among the stars. Sultan rouses Jamshed and they watch for a while before Sultan says he must take his family home.

After they've gone, Nusrat drags a wood-and-string cot out into the middle of the open courtyard beyond the persimmon tree and wraps herself in a quilt.

She thinks of the first summer after Margaret got sick, watching the meteor shower by herself in the top field on her grandfather's farm. Elaine was angry with her mother for trying to force friendships on her. All Elaine wanted was for Margaret to get better, and when that didn't happen she decided she'd rather keep to herself.

Often her mother would come out to the back yard to find Elaine making a splint out of Popsicle sticks, applying them to the leg of Pal, the family's tolerant cat, and winding gauze around the whole mess. Because Watertown provided such a safe environment for children and pets, injuries were rare. So Elaine had to pretend, and she would tie pieces of torn sheet around the middle of Gabby, the Perrins' shepherd mix. So accustomed was Gabby to Elaine's ministrations that he managed to sleep through the entire bandaging process.

Her mother tried to talk to her about making friends.

"Why don't you invite that new girl home to have lunch with you?" she asked more than once, handing over a glass of lemonade or a plate of cookies that she'd brought out into the garden with her.

One day Elaine sat in the tire swing that hung by a thick hemp rope tied to a high branch of the maple tree that shaded most of the back garden. She explained to her mother that none of the other girls enjoyed doing the things she liked to do.

"What things?" her mother asked.

"Do you remember when Margaret and I used to sit in the apple trees in Grandpa's orchard?" she asked. "We used to eat sour apples with chunks of salt chipped from the salt blocks. We had favorite cows, and we'd drop apples down for the ones we liked best. We'd see who could tell the scariest story, like about the bull chained over in the corner of the next field and how he'd run us down and grind us into fertilizer under his hooves."

Her mother tried to tell her that Margaret was gone and that she would have to learn to do things with other people. But Elaine continued to long for her sister, and so she spent many nights alone with her grandfather's telescope watching the stars. Instead of making friends she volunteered at the animal shelter. Until she met Faiz she felt nobody but Margaret—including her mother—had ever gotten to know her. As a graduate student at Columbia, when she worked full-time in her first teaching job, she found time for a second job at the West Side Animal Shelter on Ninth Avenue.

Faiz complained that she didn't have enough time for him, but even though they had fallen in love she refused to compromise. That was when he'd given her the name Nusrat, which means "Help."

5

*H*abib is a sweet baby with dark hair that stands up on end, like the reeds among the eddies on the bank of the Baba Darya. We should have cut his hair on the eighth day after his birth, but my mother insisted that we wait for Baba-jan and Nur to return. Habib's little mouth is pink and full, and his lips suck in and out when he sleeps, as if he dreams of his next meal. His eyes open wide when he awakens, and his little fists beat the air as he demands to be fed.

When Habib is nearly two weeks old, my mother and I decide I should take the goats and sheep back up into the mountains to graze. Bibi Usmani's brother and his family have not come, and my mother and I have decided we will stay, as Baba-jan wished. It's autumn, and the nights are growing colder. But the drought has held, and the sun shines with such ferocity that the dry earth rises up and floats on the air in clouds, shimmering like water in pools among the hills. The goats have eaten all of the grass I've been able to cut, and still they're so thin their ribs stick out from their bodies like kettles. The vegetables are nearly gone, and we have no ground wheat for bread. Soon we will depend on the animals alone for food, and I cannot carry enough grass to fatten them for winter.

I awake with the sun on the morning I plan to take them back into the hills. My mother and Habib sleep peacefully under a quilt on a cot beside mine. I stretch my arms over my head and wonder where Baba-jan and Nur are this morning. Then I hear someone moving about outside, and my heart leaps into my mouth. I am certain the Pashtun talib have returned to steal the animals.

I get up and walk silently on the balls of my feet to the wall at the end of the house, where I've left Baba-jan's large, curved knife that I use to cut wheat and grass. I creep to the purdah with it clutched in my hand and push aside the curtain just far enough to see Uncle Mohiuddin standing with his back to the house.

Uncle has one hand behind him, and the other is raised to shade his eyes. The way he scans the hills interlayered with mist is the same way Baba-jan looked out over his land each morning. It angers me to see Uncle behave as though our land were his. In the last two weeks Uncle has visited my mother and me more times than he has come during my entire lifetime.

It might be more accurate to say he has visited the farm. He seldom speaks to Mada-jan or to me. He simply walks around the animal pens and out to the garden plot, then back down the path to the village. He has not yet seen Habib, and I haven't offered to show him. When only I see Uncle I do not tell Mada-jan, as I don't want to worry her.

I push aside the curtain and step outside, holding the curved knife in one hand, the blade pointing toward the ground. Uncle turns in surprise.

"I thought it was the Pashtun talib," I say. "I don't want them to steal the animals." I bite the insides of my cheeks. I hadn't meant to mention the animals. Uncle laughs, his round belly wobbling under his tunic.

"Are you going to kill the Taliban?" he asks. "Do you think that will bring back your father and brother?" He laughs some more. My anger heats even more to think he finds it funny that Baba-jan and Nur have been taken away, while he has managed to stay behind. I hate him for thinking my mother and I would run away, so that he might steal our land. I barely manage to say nothing more.

But I do not ask him inside, where my mother has just gone back to sleep after feeding Habib. And I do not put down Baba-jan's knife because I don't want him to think he is welcome. Having Uncle hover about the house, especially at this early hour, makes me very uncomfortable. He paces back and forth, gazing up at the hills and out over the valley. I stand watching him, as if to say he won't get our land without a struggle from me.

A few minutes later I hear Habib cry, and my mother comes outside with him wrapped in a shawl in her arms. She does not see Uncle at first, as she hands me a cloth bag filled with bread, almonds, and dried apricots for my trip up Koh-i-Dil.

"You'd better leave early," she says, "and find a good place to spend the night." Uncle turns to face her, his back toward the path that leads down the hill to the woodpile and farther along to the Baba Darya and the village.

My mother sees him and calls out "Ho!" Uncle walks toward us and she greets him properly. "Ah-salaam-aleikum! Why do you pace so far from your brother's house? Come. Sit, and I will bring you tea." She gives me a quick look, and I take the cloth bag from my shoulder and lay it with the knife against the corner of the house.

My uncle sits on the Turkoman carpet in front of the house, and my mother unwraps Habib for him to examine while I go inside to bring cups for tea. The only thing to eat is some naan in a basket, and three amrud, which have ripened in the time since Baba-jan has gone. I pause before placing the golden fruit on a plate with the bread that I have left for my mother's breakfast.

"Najmah!" my mother calls out. I hide one amrud and a piece of bread under a cloth so my mother will have something to eat. I bring the rest out on the plate, placing it on the carpet before Uncle, who sits gazing at Habib. My mother holds the baby out to him, and pushes aside the shawl so Uncle might have a better look. Habib returns his gaze. Uncle recoils when he sees the shiny red mark where the blackened cord has fallen from Habib's belly, and I have to turn my back so that Uncle cannot see my laughter.

After Uncle has consumed the amrud and all of the bread on the plate, as well as two cups of tea, he smacks his lips, wipes the back of his hand across his mouth, and belches. My mother and I sit respectfully across from him, offering more tea and food, although there is nothing left to eat in the house—and despite his having as much food at home as he will need for the winter, I think bitterly. But I say nothing.

Finally he says, "So. Everyone is gone. You will need someone to protect you."

"My husband will come back," my mother says. "Until then Najmah and I will manage." She slides her eyes over toward me, and I feel she has read my mind. Uncle has never appeared when we needed help before. Where was he when the Taliban came? And why had they not forced him to go with them and the rest of the village men?

"Who will plant your fields?" he asks, tilting his head back so that he looks down his nose at us through slit eyes.

"The fields are planted," my mother says, lifting her chin, and returns his look with steady eyes. "We don't need help."

Uncle laughs then, his belly bouncing up and down and air hissing through his teeth.

"What did my brother plant?" he asks. "Onions?" He laughs again and smacks his fat thigh with his broad hand. "You need a crop that will produce income."

"My husband would rather burn money than grow poppies," says my mother. "We have plenty of vegetables planted. With water from the Baba Darya our autumn crops will be good. We will be fine until Salim returns. I thank you for coming to see your nephew," she says then, wrapping Habib back in his shawl in a way that lets Uncle know it is time for him to leave.

Shortly after Uncle disappears down the path, I pick up the knife and wrap it in my quilt along with the bag of fruit, bread, and nuts my mother has packed for my journey. I tie the entire large bundle to my back with a chadr and set off up the trail, turning to wave one last time to my mother and Habib.

I no longer think of leopards at all. I am more worried about leaving my mother and baby brother alone in the house with the possibility that the Taliban might return looking for more food.

I walk slowly and steadily uphill. The animals surround me, their pointed hooves stirring the dust into the air, where it hovers long after we pass. The sky holds no clouds, no breeze, no moisture. How long can this drought go on? At least the air is cool, Allah be praised.

I climb for one day and half of the next before I find enough grass to fill the animals' stomachs. When they see the grass they trot toward it eagerly and press their noses to the ground. Their hunger touches me. Animals are so trusting: they follow me anywhere, believing that I will provide for them. I am happy not to have let them down.

That night I lie on my back wrapped in my quilt, my arms behind my head, staring at the sky and thinking about where under these very same stars, this very same sky, Baba-jan and my brother might be, and whether what Uncle said was true about a battle between the Americans and the Taliban. I try hard not to think of Baba-jan and Nur without weapons pitted against American bombs, but my heart thumps dully in my chest and I realize that's all I can think about.

I search the sky for the pattern of stars that make the gazelle, which sometimes turns into a fish. In the mountains we are nearer the stars, and they shine brightly in brilliant colors. I feel as if I might reach out and touch some of the closer ones. Baba-jan told Nur and me many stories about each cluster of stars, so that the stories became confused in our minds. He told us the gazelle, which is difficult to see because it's so shy, will bring good luck in the form of a gentle rain that might last several days. Sometimes in her effort to evade us, the gazelle will turn into a fish or a goat. Nur and I often pursued her through the night sky—seeing her just as she disappeared behind a cloud or another cluster of stars—until we fell asleep.

As I watch the sky the stars begin to move and

leap, so that I sit up and rub my eyes, thinking they are playing tricks on me. After a while it seems the night is alive with light—arcs of yellow, blue, and green that cut across the darkness. I have never seen such bursts of light—so many lines going in every direction—I can find nothing among the stars that I recognize. Are the Americans shooting the stars out of the sky? I lie awake the rest of the night in terror, with the stars exploding in a heaven that seems close enough to touch.

I doze just before dawn and awake with a start to see the thin turquoise line that draws the shape of the mountains against low, lavender clouds. The sky looks just as it does every morning when the sun prepares to rise over Kunduz. For a moment I believe I have only dreamed of the exploding stars. I rub my eyes and arise.

All around me the animals graze peacefully, and the only sound is the tearing of dry grass between their teeth. Although I have been gone only two days, I decide to stay one more day and then leave the animals to graze while I return home to check on my mother and Habib.

I sleep soundly that night. The one time I awake, the sky is black, with the stars brilliant, white, and still—reassuring in the distance as they have been forever. In the morning I descend Koh-i-Dil quickly.

Coming down takes only half a day, a third of the time it takes to climb up.

As I come around the side of the hill on the path, I see my mother far below, shaking out the quilts and laying them to air across the legs of the overturned cots. Habib sleeps in a little sling made by a chadr strung between the widespread arms of the acacia tree at the end of the garden. My mother straightens her back and lifts her hand to shade her eyes. I think perhaps she's seen me coming along the path and wonders why I've come back early. But she is looking up at the sky, where in the distance a white trail is visible behind an arrow-shaped phantom high, high against the blue, crossing the sky from west to east. And then I hear a strange whistling sound that seems to grow louder, and the ground heaves and a loud thump echoes from somewhere below. The village, I think, and begin to run.

My mother must have had the same thought. She moves quickly, scooping Habib up from his hammock and running toward the open doorway of the house. She looks back over her shoulder and sees me, running now down the path. We look at each other for the briefest instant, our tongues locked inside our mouths.

By then the explosions are closer and louder. They feel as if they're happening inside my own chest.

The wind has picked up, so that it's difficult to see for the dust. I know I cannot make it to the house, and I run to hide among the boulders alongside the path. The ground jumps crazily beneath me, and I lose my footing. As I fall I pull the bundle of my quilt wrapped inside my chadr on top of me. Slivers and chunks of rock shoot out around me and then clatter down like hail. After the deafening thumps and roaring of the explosions, suddenly I hear nothing. My ears feel as if someone has clapped them hard, and the pressure in my head is terrible. I try to draw air into my chest, but it will not expand.

When I am able to sit—I can't say how much later—I am behind the boulders, just where I fell. Everything is still, and dust hangs heavily in the air. My ears ring, and it takes me a few moments to collect myself and stand. I run then toward home, but when I reach the path and look down I recognize nothing. A few timbers stand where our house was just moments before. A layer of coarse dust lies on the acacia tree where Habib lay hammocked in my mother's chadr, which hangs now shredded into wisps, recognizable only by their soft gray color. The path is an indentation that meanders under the dust from behind where the house stood to the lip of the hill.

I stumble toward the broken upright timbers of

the doorframe and the chunks of mud plaster and dust scattered over the footprint of what was my home. My mother lies on the ground nearby with her legs splayed at odd angles to the rest of her. She reaches her hand toward me, and opens her lips to speak. Instead of words, blood pours from her mouth. By the time I reach her she stares with glassy, dead eyes. Habib lies motionless a few feet behind her, facedown in the dirt, his little arms flung out to his sides in the way he throws them wide when he lies naked on the cot swimming for joy in the fresh air.

6

*U*nder the persimmon tree in Nusrat's garden six children sit on three wood-and-string cots drawn together into the shape of a U. On the cot in the center are Fariel, who Nusrat thinks is about ten, and her younger sister, Tahira. The two girls have long, faded scarves draped over their heads, the ends flung back limply over their shoulders. Four boys sit on two cots arranged at right angles to the girls' cot.

Nusrat stands before the children, who are refugees from Afghanistan, and points with a long stick to a large chalkboard balanced on a tripod as they recite their five times tables. It's late morning, and the boys have begun to lose their concentration.

Ahmed, the tallest of the four boys, stares at Nusrat, his eyes never wavering from hers, as if he has never in his life seen anything quite as blue as her irises. Beside Ahmed sits his brother, Wali, the youngest boy, who squirms as if he has worms under his skin. Across from them sit Farooq and Farid, another pair of brothers, who have been poking each other for several minutes when they think Nusrat's blue eyes cannot see their mischief.

The children were shepherds in Afghanistan, and the boys in particular had difficulty sitting in one place for more than a few minutes when they'd first come to Nusrat's Persimmon Tree School. She has been teaching them the poetry of numbers, and about the dance of the planets and stars in the heavens. They're better now about sitting still, but in comparison to the children Nusrat taught in America, these are a challenge.

"Tomorrow," Nusrat says, "we will talk about the number six. It's one of those magical numbers that are called 'perfect numbers,' and we will talk about why that's so. Now it's time to wash our hands for lunch." With that there is a juicy *plop* as a ripe persimmon drops from the tree, its skin a rich, mel-

low orange. Even before the sound of the fruit landing, it seems, the four boys sitting on the cots with
their feet dangling over the side scramble in a cloud
of dust. Farooq, a tall, scrappy boy, emerges from the
cloud and holds the persimmon high over his head in
victory, the other boys jumping for it to grab it away.

"You may each have a persimmon after you've
eaten," Nusrat says. "Husna will bring your lunch in
just a minute." The others stare at Farooq with large
dark eyes as he eats the puckery orange custard of the
fruit hungrily. Intent concentration makes a mask of
his face as sweet orange juice makes a trail in the dust
down his brown arm, and the other boys' eyes shift to
follow its progress.

Husna scurries from the back of the bungalow with a large tray balanced on one shoulder. On
the tray are stacked aluminum tumblers, a sweating
metal pitcher, metal plates, a tray of spiced goat meat
kebabs, and a basket of fragrant white slabs of flat
bread, steam curling up into the sunlit air.

Nusrat drags a rough wooden table into the
space in the center of the wood-and-string cots, and
Husna sets the tray on it, then straightens to tuck a
strand of graying hair behind her ear before taking
the plates of kebabs and naan from the tray and setting them on the table. She fills the tumblers with fil-
tered water from the sweating metal pitcher.

At a back corner of the outside kitchen wall the children crowd around a painted metal stand that holds a basin of water. They nudge each other aside to scrub the dirt from their hands, drying them on a worn pink towel before coming to the table. Nusrat hands each of them a plate, and they grab for the spicy meat and the still-warm bread, jostling each other in a chaotic ritual they perform each day.

The children sit again on the cots in the same formation as before, swinging their feet contentedly, eating from their plates with their fingers, the chickens scratching in the dirt under the cots.

At the blue-painted back gate a bell rings, and Nusrat crosses the dusty garden to peer over the wall that surrounds the property to see Haroon, the malek of the Shahnawaz refugee camp, standing beside the gate in a white turban with a long tail hanging down his back, a dark green jacket with a broken zipper, and dusty sandals on his feet. Beside him stand a thin little girl in a short, faded dress and a woman in a tattered blue burqa. The child wears no shoes, and her feet and ankles and calves are the color of the dust in the lane. She shivers slightly in the cool autumn air, despite the warmth of sunlight. Her hair is bleached a dull, reddish blond by malnutrition. Under her burqa the mother stands completely motionless, her head bent forward as if she stares at the ground.

Nusrat opens the gate and greets them all. "Ah-salaam-aleikum. Come in, come in," she says. "You are just in time for dinner!"

"Waleikum ah-salaam," Haroon responds. "Sorry to bother you at your meal." He is a sturdy man of medium build with a graying beard and mustache and kind eyes. "This is Mansoora, a widow from Jalalabad, and her daughter, Amina. Do you have room for the girl in your class?"

"Welcome," says Nusrat, reaching out for Amina's shoulder to guide her inside the gate. "Please, come in!" She smiles at the widow, whose eyes won't come up from the ground to meet Nusrat's.

"Please don't let us disturb you . . ." Haroon says, but Nusrat knows by the way the widow hangs her head that she hasn't had a meal in a long time. Nusrat has learned from her husband and his family that Afghans never let anyone go away hungry if they can manage it.

"No, I insist!" she says. "We have plenty to eat. Come in." Mansoora's hand comes out from under the folds of her burqa, and she touches her forehead in a gesture more of gratitude than greeting. Her fingernails are rimed with dirt, and the hands are hatched with dry white cracks like the hands of an old woman.

Nusrat beckons to Husna and leans close to ask

her to feed Mansoora in the kitchen and give her a basket of food to take home. "I've seen that woman begging in the lane near the Chota Bazaar," says Husna under her breath. "All I could see was her bare hand, and it was filthy."

"Never mind, Husna," says Nusrat. "Just take her to the bathroom and give her soap and a towel. The poor soul probably hasn't had a good wash or a meal in longer than I care to think about." Husna mutters to herself as she crosses the courtyard to the kitchen door.

"Won't you stay, too?" Nusrat asks Haroon. "We have plenty." But Haroon never stays.

"Thank you, memsaheb," he says, and touches his forehead with his fingertips before backing through the gate.

Haroon found each of Nusrat's students in the refugee camp. He brought them one or two at a time, beginning the first day the school was open, the spring before—early, when the sweet peas climbed the strings that the gardener had hung from the wall. Sweet peas are Nusrat's favorite flower. Their purple, pink, and white fragrance slips in through her shuttered windows on early spring mornings.

First Haroon came to the back gate with Farooq and Farid, who are brothers only a year or so apart in age, although they are nearly the same size. Nusrat's

Dari was not as good in those days, and she thought the children had come to study, as she'd arranged with Haroon. The truth was that the boys' mother had heard a rich foreign lady lived in the house with the huge persimmon tree in its garden, and they'd come looking for food. Nusrat promised to feed the boys if they'd stay and learn their numbers.

Next came Fariel and Tahira, whose father had been killed by the Taliban, leaving their mother a young widow. And a few weeks later came Ahmed and his brother, Wali. Other children had come and gone as families found relatives in other camps and their fortunes changed. Nusrat guessed the children were aged between eight and eleven. They could not tell her exactly, because shepherds tended not to pay much attention to such details as birth dates. They were much more likely to remember occurrences in terms of their proximity to wars and earthquakes and droughts and floods.

Every day the authorities in Peshawar hand out more yellow UN food packets and ration cards to keep the refugees from starving. The farmers harvest their meager crops and sell them to merchants who haul them on trucks to the markets in the cities near the refugee camps. But the stalls always seem empty. Nusrat has heard that the Taliban steal the trucks and the food that's in them before they ever reach the cities. For her own kitchen she grows fruit and vegetables and shops directly from farmers who bring eggs, milk, chickens, and produce from their land at the outskirts of the city.

The children's mothers give them tea before setting off for Nusrat's school each morning. At noon Nusrat feeds them a meal with meat and bread and vegetables, much more than their mothers eat the entire day. And when the mothers return to fetch the children in the afternoons, the teacher fills their baskets with persimmons from the tree, freshly baked naan, and vegetables and herbs from her lovingly kept garden plot at the side of the house.

The summer has been dry, the fifth year in a stubborn drought, and although the planted rows are even and neat, the sturdy small plants shine with the iridescence of fine white dust. Nusrat and Husna help the gardener, whom they share with Asma's family, to haul water from the river for the garden. Husna is protective of her American memsaheb, whom she regards as very foolish, feeding everyone and his cousin from her garden that they work so hard to keep alive.

Nusrat is wealthy only by the standards of Peshawar, but to those who have so little her wealth is prodigious. She reels the children in like fish: she lures their bodies with food and their spirits with stories about the stars. It's their minds she's after, for she knows that without some education these children will be lost forever. She's determined to turn their time of greatest need into a time of opportunity.

After the meal, Nusrat leads Amina to the cot where Tahira and Fariel sit. They scoot together to make room for her on the end near Farooq and Farid. Dried mucus is caked under Amina's nose, and she stares at the other two girls. She has eaten almost nothing, although Nusrat knows she must be hungry. Mucus rattles in the child's chest. Fariel and Tahira avoid touching her as if they know all about contagious respiratory illnesses.

"This afternoon," Nusrat begins after they're settled, "we will talk more about time and space. Last week we talked about a star that exploded 160,000 monsoons ago. The star was so far away that we're just now seeing the explosion. Does anyone have a question?" Farid stands.

"Uncle says this is wrong." He speaks so quietly Nusrat can barely hear him. "He says this is an un-Islamic idea."

"It is neither an Islamic idea nor an un-Islamic one," says Nusrat. "It's science. But the Koran has great wisdom about the heavens and how they expand, even though it came long ago. People who didn't know what was in the Koran invented myths to explain what they couldn't understand. Do you remember what myth is?"

Wali jumps up and down in his seat. "Yes, Wali?" says Nusrat.

"Myth is a story, like the story about the demon star that is the eye of the monster with snakes in her hair," Wali says proudly. Of all the children, he loves the star stories most.

"Yes!" says Nusrat. "The star is called 'demon' because its light is unpredictable—it's a story invented to explain what at that time was unexplainable."

Nusrat draws a diagram of the planets around the sun, and she gives the children pieces of chalk to draw on the small wooden chalkboards that rest on their laps. She calls Husna from the garden and beckons her to come closer. As the children draw, she whispers close to Husna's ear.

"Please go to Dr. Naveed's clinic. Wait there for me. Tell him I will bring a sick child with me when school is finished. We will not be much longer." Husna nods and goes to fetch her burqa from the house. But Nusrat can tell by the set of Husna's mouth that she does not approve.

After the children have gone, Nusrat has no difficulty persuading Mansoora and Amina to stay behind. Mansoora stares at the ground while Nusrat explains that Amina has something wrong with her chest.

"Do you understand?" Nusrat asks the girl's mother. Mansoora nods her head slowly. "So," Nusrat continues, "we will take her to the doctor and he will give her some medicine. We'll buy her a shawl and some shoes so she can keep warm. The cold weather is coming." Mansoora doesn't reply, but she doesn't object.

Nusrat goes out to the tonga queue at the end of the street and hires Basharat and his small tonga cart drawn by two thin horses to take them to Dr. Naveed's clinic. Dr. Naveed lives just down the street, but his clinic is about a mile away, where it is convenient to the refugee camps. Nusrat uses Basharat whenever she goes to the bazaar, or the clinic, or to visit Faiz's family in University Town.

Basharat treats his horses well and is extremely trustworthy. Nusrat pays him a small retainer to be available when she and Husna need him. Most households employ men as servants, but many foreigners prefer women. The disadvantage to having a female servant is that many women are not comfortable going to the bazaar unless they are accompanied by a close male relative. Basharat poses as the brother or husband of Nusrat or Husna, who of course wear burqas whenever they leave the house. Women also are discouraged from making purchases from male shopkeepers, so Basharat makes their purchases for a small percentage. Usually the tonga driver's son accompanies them so they're less likely to be questioned by the Taliban, whose influence is strong even in Peshawar, where the majority of residents—both Afghan and Pakistani—are Pashtu speakers.

Nusrat and Mansoora and Amina climb into the cart and sit facing backward, watching the traffic close in behind them. Basharat's son, who is about ten years old, sits beside his father on the driver's seat.

Most of the traffic consists of motorized cycle rickshaws that bleat like angry goats and send up noxious fumes and donkey-drawn carts filled with used clothing and machine parts, steel reinforcement rods, pots and pans, and all kinds of goods bound for the bazaar.

Basharat skirts the bazaar, which is at the center of a complex of lanes that radiate outward like the spokes of a wheel. The thoroughfare that makes a ring at the rim of the wheel is too crowded for vehicles to pass through during the day.

Nusrat turns in her seat and notices two bareheaded men running from the gate at the main lane leading from the bazaar. Over the bobbing red pom-

pom plumes attached to the horses' bridles she sees other men running, several of them wearing dark turbans. These men carry guns. She has barely had time to wonder what the commotion is about when a terrible explosion thunders down the lane from the center of the bazaar, pushing dust, smoke, and scraps of papers along the alleys like puffs of smoke through a pipe.

Basharat jumps from the cart to the ground, his son right behind him. The horses dance and rear, their eyes sliding sideways, and Basharat grabs their bridles before they can gallop away and overturn the cart. "Turn around," Nusrat shouts at him. "Take us back! Zut! Zut!" Bombs are not unusual in the bazaar, but she is afraid that gunfire will follow, as it often does.

Basharat motions for the women to get out of the tonga. Nusrat lifts Amina to the ground and then helps Mansoora. The horses jostle and bump each other as Basharat turns them in the narrow lane. He motions his son to get on the side of the cart where Nusrat stands with Mansoora and Amina, with the cart between them and the commotion. Masses of panicked animals and humans and small vehicles close in around them, blocking the thoroughfare as everyone in the street tries to turn back. People abandon draft animals and vehicles and run away on foot.

Nusrat decides to stay with Basharat, and she grabs a hand on either side of her, afraid Amina and Mansoora might try to run away. Basharat's son stands bravely in front of them as if he is their sole protector. A few shots ring out, and Basharat motions them to get under the cart. The horses dance nervously, but Basharat stands between them, holding their bridles.

The shooting ends as quickly as it has begun, with the armed men running down alleys and disappearing without a trace. Nusrat crawls out from under the cart and helps Mansoora to her feet. Amina stands behind her mother and peers out with eyes that are large and frightened.

Basharat and Nusrat decide they might as well go on to Dr. Naveed's clinic, since the troublemakers have run in the direction of Nusrat's house and the clinic is in the opposite direction. They all climb back into the cart and go on, hoping Basharat has chosen a safe route. They pass the police, who run down the lane toward the bazaar too late.

Nusrat thinks how easily violence happens here, how quickly it passes, with everyone acting as if everything is normal soon afterward. Her mind flies to Faiz, and she wonders again where he might be and whether he is safe.

NAJMAH

Golestan Village, Kunduz Province,
Northern Afghanistan

7

I turn Habib over. He is lifeless, his small body heavy and still. His eyes are closed, and dust covers every inch of him. My mother kept him so clean, but now mud cakes in the saliva drying around his mouth. My heart hammers as if it wants to escape my chest, and it is the only sound I hear apart from the heavy ringing in my ears.

I hold Habib close, as if the warmth of my body will bring him back to life. I can tell by his utter stillness that he is gone. I carry him to where my mother lies on her side, her arm still outstretched toward the path where I ran down the hill. I place him in the curve of her elbow and brush her dark hair back from her face, tucking a strand behind her ear, as she has done with my hair a thousand times, without my ever thinking about it once.

I sit in the dirt beside them quietly, not crying, not thinking, not even aware that I am breathing, and it occurs to me that I might be dead, too. I must have sat for a long time, although I have no recollection of the time passing. The sun is nearing the rim of Koh-i-Dil when I hear the dull sound of an animal's hoof strike a rock and the squeak of leather against wood. It's the first I am aware I can hear again, and I notice that a bitter chill has settled in the early evening air. I do not run or try to hide. I don't care whether the Taliban find me and kill me.

The next thing I am conscious of is being lifted in the arms of Bibi Usmani's brother Akhtar, who carries me across what was the front of our house to the broken acacia tree. Akhtar's wife, Khalida, cups my chin in her hand and pours water into my mouth from a ladle. Khalida wears men's clothing.

She tears up pieces of cloth and pours water over them, using them to wipe blood and caked dirt from my face. She does not try to talk to me, and I am grateful. What can anyone say to me now? I lie very still on a pile of quilts that Akhtar has taken from the back of their donkey, and I watch Khalida move in and out of my vision. I do not resist—nor do I help—when she removes the remains of my tunic and skirt, which have been shredded by shards of flying rock in the bombing. She dabs the damp cloths over the cuts and bruises on my body.

Out near the edge of the hill, beside the path that leads down to the Baba Darya, I hear the clang of a shovel striking rock-hard earth.

Khalida pushes my arms into a man's tunic, and she tugs a pair of trousers up over my hips, pulling the drawstring until it's snug against my waist. She holds out her hands to me, and I take them. She pulls me to my feet and looks at me, her head tilted to one side.

Akhtar digs steadily, his shovel pulverizing the red dirt, which scatters like dust as he flings it aside. The light of the setting sun makes sparkles of the particles that still hang in the air.

Khalida gently turns my face back toward her and holds out my long hair to the sides of my face. She picks up a pair of scissors that lies on the pile of quilts and snips at my hair in short strokes until it bristles out all over my head. When she has finished, she and Akhtar gather up my hair. They sprinkle it into the large hole Akhtar has dug in the ground and then he fills the hole with dirt. Afterward Akhtar shakes out a length of striped gray silk and winds a turban over my cropped head. He hands me a pair of new brown leather sandals.

"These will be too large," he says, "but you should wear them anyway. We will walk through the mountains, where there is snow, and these will protect you. You will be safer dressed as a boy traveling through strange areas." I obey without thinking, and when I have slipped the rough hard leather over my feet he boosts me up on top of the quilts, which he's piled again on the donkey's back. I ride through most of the night with Akhtar and Khalida's two small sons clinging to me. Throughout the night I am aware of nothing except that it is cold and the only warmth comes from the boys' arms holding tightly around my middle, and the little donkey swaying as he makes his gentle way behind Akhtar, who walks. Khalida rides a camel that plods behind us.

It isn't until the first tinge of light shows on the horizon that I realize the hole where Akhtar has buried my hair also holds my mother and baby brother. I look back over my shoulder at the path we've ridden all through the night. But they are far, far behind us, and I realize I will never see them again.

As the stars disappear one by one, Akhtar leads us away from the path and down into a valley formed by a small stream that flows into a larger river. Pine trees nestle beside the stream, and the donkey trots toward the water, lowering his head to drink when he's still several feet away. Akhtar rouses his two sons, who sleep leaning against each other, and both of them against me. He sets them gently on their feet and then helps me to the ground.

In the sharp light of the rising sun our breath puffs out in front of us as Khalida and I spread quilts on the ground. I am stiff and weary, and the many bruises on my arms and legs ache and throb, but I don't want to sleep. I am afraid if I close my eyes I'll see my mother's outstretched arm and the stain of blood spreading around her and Habib's perfect small body, both of them still and covered with dust. Khalida gives me some bread, which I refuse.

"You must eat," she says. "Even if you don't want to. We will sleep today and walk again tomorrow. Akhtar will get food at the bazaar for the rest of the journey. You and I must take turns walking and riding." She holds the bread out again, and I take it. When I have eaten it she gives me some nuts and dried plums, and we all drink water.

The air warms, and Khalida, the children, and I sleep on and off during the day. I hear Akhtar lead the donkey away, and I awake to the sound of Khalida and Akhtar whispering after he returns. Khalida wakes me, and we eat more stale naan and tea.

"I don't want this," says one of the little boys, handing his bread back to his mother.

"Shush," she says, not unkindly. "Baba-jan was not able to get anything more to eat at the bazaar. We'll have to wait until the next place. For now it's all there is. Eat it or you will be hungry." The little boy takes the bread back and holds it in his fist, staring into the fire.

The next morning we arise before the sun after sleeping without dreaming, huddled together for warmth on the cold ground. The pine trees wear red haloes of dust as the orange sun climbs the cold, still sky. We wind our way down the little stream's valley until we come to another large river, which twists like a snake through the hills. We turn our backs to the sun and follow the flat gray water along a bed of round river rocks that make my feet twist and turn in the new chappals. Without asking Akhtar, I take them off and strap them together, slinging them over my shoulder. My feet are tough from years of wandering after the sheep and goats along the rim of Koh-i-Dil.

Whenever we're hungry we drink water. The nuts and dried apricots are gone. The bread is moldy. The first day my stomach growls, but after that I no longer feel hungry.

On the third day we come to a large town. I have

not spoken once on our journey, although Khalida and Akhtar have been kind to me. They speak to me and try to make me feel welcome. But I feel as if my tongue has been locked inside my mouth since the moment I saw my mother airing the quilts just before the bombs fell. I try to communicate, but although the words form inside my head, my tongue and lips will not cooperate. I try to show that I'm grateful by helping with the little boys and the animals.

Women sit along parts of the main thoroughfare of the town, only their hands visible, sticking out from under their burqas, their fingernails broken and split, begging for coins. Dirty, naked children with swollen bellies and noses caked with mucus shout hoarsely as they play on the walkway behind the women. They seem oblivious to the cold, but I'm sure they feel its sting just as I do.

"They'll never make it," mutters Khalida, who walks beside me, leading the camel. I lead the donkey, and the two boys ride. Khalida doesn't look like a man—more like a boy with a thin face. She, too, has cropped her hair and wears a striped gray turban wound over it. Just seconds after Khalida speaks, a black-turbaned talib comes along with a bamboo stave and whacks at the legs of the poor women begging along the road. They help each other to their feet under the blows of his cane, which makes a whistling sound as it passes through the air before thwacking against their long robes and legs.

I look up at Khalida and our eyes lock for a second, then she looks away, and I do the same. But my heart races. Several of the women carry babies wrapped in the folds of their robes, some no older than Habib. It exhausts me to think what might have happened to their husbands, and it makes me imagine that terrible things have happened to Baba-jan and Nur. I can't think of anything else. It isn't until later that I wonder how the women will feed their children, and how they can walk over the mountains in the snow and cold to the border if they don't have food.

At the end of the street we come to a well where several other large thoroughfares like the one we've been walking along come together. Akhtar leaves Khalida and me at the well to look after the donkey, the camel, and the two little boys while he goes into the bazaar once again to search for food.

"This may be the last water until we get to Torkhum," Akhtar says as he leaves us. "Fill every pot."

I long to go with him because I think perhaps I'll see Baba-jan and my brother, or hear something about them. But Khalida's eyes are frightened, like those of a donkey that's being mistreated. She seems unable to move, and so I unload the animals, piling all of our belongings beside the well, where a man is watering his sheep. When Khalida doesn't try to help, I find the water pots and unlash them and look among the quilts where I saw her bury the goatskin bucket the day before.

Khalida moves closer to where I stand beside the camel's shoulder and turns her back to the shepherd, who pays no attention to us. She holds me firmly by the shoulders and leans forward to whisper into my ear.

"If you speak," she says, her voice barely audible, "be sure to call me Khalid. Not Khalida. I shall call you Shaheed." I nod my head slightly. "It isn't safe for a woman or girl in a strange city," she whispers, shifting her chin toward where the Pashtun talib had beaten the women begging by the side of the street. Their places have been taken by elderly men whose hands stretch out as the women's hands had done, hoping for money or food.

Suddenly I understand. Since I'm not quite of an age when I must cover my head, I am used to looking at the world unhampered by yards and yards of fabric. Khalida is used to being invisible under a burqa to shield her from the eyes of strangers whenever she leaves her house. Even though she looks like a boy of about the same age as Nur, she doesn't feel comfortable without the veil.

But nobody bothers to look at us. A herd of goats passes by, and donkeys laden with loads of wood. Their owners walk past without noticing us. Uzbek merchants hurry along the street in striped silk robes, the extravagantly long sleeves slung back over their shoulders. They wear high, soft leather boots. Their faces are flat and their eyes have no creases in the lids.

When the shepherd and his flock move away from the well, I pick up the end of the rope that's strung through a pulley on the stanchion that stands over the well and fasten it to the donkey's harness. I tie the other end to the goatskin and drop it into the well, then lead the donkey away, hauling the full goatskin bucket to the surface. I empty the water from the goatskin repeatedly into the concrete trough around the well and let the animals drink. A stray dog, thin and scarred and covered with ticks, joins them. I let them all drink their fill, then attach the rope once again and fill our metal water pots.

Khalida stands hugging herself in the meager shade of a dead tree trunk and watches the boys as they chase each other around the well. She shivers, but I am warm from working. A few times she calls them back when they've gone too far up one of the streets that sprawl away from the well.

When I have finished, I bring her a cup of water. We rest a few moments, and then Khalida and I re-load the donkey. We move to sit in the sun at the foot of a wall across the street to watch the boys and wait for Akhtar.

NUSRAT
Peshawar, Pakistan

8

Nusrat helps Husna clean up the kitchen. They finish just before the electricity is switched off, and Nusrat automatically reaches for matches to light one of the two kerosene lamps on the kitchen table beside the window that looks out over the garden. She says good night to Husna and takes one of the lamps to her room, which looks strange to her after the violent events of the afternoon. Her shawl is draped over the back of the chair in front of her desk, and her pen lies where she left it across the writing tablet as if she'd just interrupted herself in the act of writing the letter she sent off to Faiz in the morning.

She sets the lamp on the desk and sits down in the chair where she'd written the note. She stares into the flame in the chimney of the lamp and imagines his face. When she thinks of him these days she remembers him smiling, although she thinks possibly there is little reason for him to smile very often now. Faiz is not a fearful man, but he knows he can't be of help to the people he's working among if he's dead. He would take care of himself and be cautious. Nusrat catches herself rubbing her hands together hard, as if she's washing something terrible from them.

If only they'd stayed in New York as they'd planned, she thinks. But no—she doesn't really mean that. She loves being here with him. She loves him even more than she loved him when they married, because he couldn't keep from coming back when he thought his people needed him.

It had happened about a year after they married. The news from Afghanistan had been troubling for some time, but more frequent stories reached them of attacks on innocent people by Taliban goon squads. Nusrat began to notice that Faiz seemed distracted and withdrawn. She tried to get him to talk about what was on his mind.

"Have you ever had something happen to a member of your family that you thought you might have been able to do something about?" he asked one morning as they sat on the sofa in their living room drinking coffee. Sun streamed in through the window, and the old brass samovar on the table behind Faiz's head glowed warmly.

"No, I have not," she said. "But your family are okay. Aren't they? Nothing has happened to anyone in your family, has it?"

"Not just my family," Faiz said, "it's the whole country. I feel helpless, and at the same time I know that I could help."

"Well," said Nusrat, pausing only briefly, and rushing on before she could change her mind, "then why don't you help? You don't have to stay here. Is that what you want? To return to Afghanistan? What would you do there?"

They had been sitting side by side reading the Sunday *New York Times* and eating blueberry scones, a rare luxury for them because usually one of them—if not both—is at work. Faiz put down his paper and turned to her, drawing her closer to him.

"I have more than myself to think of," he said. "Now that we're married I can't just go away and leave you. Afghanistan is a very dangerous place, and my family is not without enemies in the government of the Taliban. Going there is not a thing to do lightly."

"I am your wife, Faiz," she said. "I will go with

you to Afghanistan. Of course we would take what's happening in Afghanistan very seriously."

"You mean you'd go with me?" he asked. "I never dared hope you would . . ."

"I would love to go there with you," she said. "I could stay in Peshawar with Asma and Sultan and your mother. You could come to visit. Or I would work with you if that would be a help . . ."

"A field hospital is no place for a woman," he said. "Especially an American woman."

Faiz had worked to set up rural hospitals in Afghanistan after finishing his residency at Columbia in 1994. Civil war raged in much of Afghanistan during that time, and when the Taliban became more powerful they closed the field hospitals as quickly as they were organized. Faiz returned to New York in 1997. He met Nusrat in 1999, and they married a year later.

"You are a rare person," he said, drawing her close to him and planting a kiss in her hair. "You don't just want to help. You are willing to commit yourself to what you believe."

Until she met Faiz, Nusrat had never even thought of her country as a thing that needed to be committed to.

Shortly after Faiz returned to New York a letter came from Fatima saying that Asma had been stopped in the street in front of their house in Kabul, the capital of Afghanistan. She had stepped outside the gate to meet Jamshed's van from school. Just as the van came down the street, a man in a black turban walked out of the alley that ran alongside the house. He hurried over to where Asma stood waiting while Jamshed climbed down the van's steps to the curb.

"You're in violation of the dress code," the man said to Asma. Stunned, she did not immediately answer. The Taliban had never shown up in their neighborhood before. She was not afraid because she was covered from head to foot in a burqa and the fellow looked familiar to her. "I can see the hem of your dress under your burqa," the man went on, reaching out to grab her by the arm. "It's red. That's not allowed." Asma pulled back just as she realized that this was the son of their neighbor. They had gone to the same elementary school. She hardly recognized him under his huge turban and beard.

"You're Abdur Rahman," she said, staring at him through the lattice piece in her burqa. He didn't reply, but raised the cane over his head as if to strike her. He held tightly to her wrist. Asma let out a small scream as she turned to keep the blow from falling on her head.

"You dare speak to a strange man in the street?"

he snarled, the cane still raised above his head. "Harlot! I'm taking you with me to the Ministry for the Prevention of Vice and Promotion of Virtue!"

Sultan was sitting out on the terrace in front of the house just on the other side of the wall, supervising the planting of flowers in the garden, when he heard Asma cry out. He ran to the gate and saw his wife struggling with a man in a dark turban. Jamshed stood beside them, and when he saw his father he let out a shriek and ran to him, throwing his small arms around his father's legs.

"What is this about?" Sultan demanded in his usually gentle voice. He scooped Jamshed up and set him inside the gate, then turned around to face the Pashtun talib.

"This woman has violated the dress code and is in the street talking to strange men," the man said.

"Nonsense!" said Sultan, standing up to his full height of six and a half feet. "This is my wife. We live in this house. You have no business bothering decent people in their own neighborhoods. Go away and don't come back here to bother us again."

Perhaps cowed by Sultan's size or the authority in his normally quiet voice, the man let Asma go and stared at Sultan for several seconds before walking away, muttering curses and swinging his cane, which made swishing noises as it cut through the air.

The air is thick with a pale gray dust that has settled over the remains of the town like a mist. We stop for a time to help, Akhtar digging with his shovel, and Khalida and me with our bare hands. We pull a child from the dust, spluttering and coughing. I think I should feel grateful that he has survived, even though my own baby brother did not. But these are only thoughts, with no feelings attached. His mother falls on him, crying and screaming with relief that he is alive. Other refugees keep walking on the road past the town.

As the sun begins its descent that afternoon, the headman of the village tells Akhtar we should move on.

"We have no food to give you," he says. "You should conserve your strength for your journey. We will follow behind you once everyone is accounted for." Akhtar is reluctant to leave, but there is no choice and we are under way again well before the sun sets.

By that evening a dull ache has settled into my belly and my bowels, and my legs feel as if they're made of water. I am unable to concentrate on anything, not even on how I will look for my father and brother. The thought that I might be an orphan hovers around me like a wicked djinn, and so my mind flits from one thought to another, not allowing in anything that is so troubling. The little boys cry that they are hungry, and Khalida weeps, wiping her face on the end of her turban as she walks. We don't rest until long after dark. It's cold, but I am so numb I hardly notice. I'm not aware of sleeping all night—there is no relief from the long endless pain in my stomach that won't stop no matter how much water I drink.

In the morning we have walked only a short distance when we hear a loud, rhythmic *crump*-ing in the hills around the road. We stop, and the explosions grow closer, interspersed with gunfire that sends up small spurts of dust along the roadway. People all around us dive for the shelter of rocks that lie along the sides of the road. Akhtar waves his arms at us to do the same.

Akhtar grabs the pattu shawl that lies folded across his shoulder and shakes it out as he runs to grab up his two sons. He draws the shawl around him and the boys, making a tent by draping the shawl over his head and arms, and in the same fluid motion he drops to the ground, pulling them with him. Crouching there motionless, they look like a great, dun-colored boulder. Khalida grabs me and yanks the donkey's lead from my hand, dropping it in the roadway. She pulls me with her under her pattu, and we huddle in the ditch beside the road. We also do our best to imitate a boulder.

"Don't move," Khalida whispers against the side of my cropped head. "Not a muscle!" I nod against her to let her know I understand.

Next we hear whistling and whining and the thud of explosions all around us. The noise doesn't seem so loud, but with every thud we feel the ground jump, and rock rains over us. The sound of gunfire is everywhere, and a spot between my shoulder blades begins to quiver with fear. I wonder if we have been hit and don't realize it yet—or perhaps we are already dead and we only imagine we are still alive.

Khalida holds me close to her chest, squeezing more tightly with every explosion until I'm breathless. We remain that way, our legs and backs aching, for a very long time, until I feel I can stay motionless no longer. Finally Khalida pulls back the shawl and peers out from underneath. Akhtar stands over us and holds out his hands to pull Khalida and me to our feet.

The donkey is nowhere to be found, but the camel has not wandered far off. Akhtar lashes his sons to the pile of belongings on the camel's back, and soon we are walking again. In the first few minutes we pass several dead camels, lying tied nose to tail beside the road, just as they've fallen. We also pass the bodies of people who were shot down as they ran to take cover. I peer closely at them to see whether I recognize anyone, but I do not. I don't feel anything about them at all—only a curiosity about who they are and where they come from.

That afternoon Akhtar leads us away from the road, following what looks like a goat track around a rocky hill. He comes to a stop behind a pile of boulders, where he stretches the ropes that have tied their belongings to the camel among the boulders and covers them with the shawls.

"Stay under this canopy and don't talk or move until I come back," he says to Khalida and me. I nod my head to show I understand, and he pats the top of my turban.

"Where are you going?" Khalida asks. Her voice is high-pitched, and she sounds both angry and frightened.

"Just stay hidden until I come back," Akhtar repeats.

"Please, Akhtar," Khalida pleads with him. "Don't frighten us this way. You are no longer mujahid . . ." Akhtar pulls her under the canopy.

"Get some rest, all of you," he says, gruffly. "I will look for some food." I try to imagine where he

[*106*]

will find food in these rocky hills. But I remember he fought here with the mujahideen and he knows the hills well.

"You will be fine," he says, "and I will be fine. Stay here." Khalida sits down and weeps as she watches Akhtar's back disappear up the goat track, among the boulders along the rim of the hill above us. Khalida pulls the boys closer to her, and I huddle against their backs. As the sun slides behind the hill, the air chills immediately. The camel carries the cooking pots, but we have no food. The quilts have disappeared with the donkey, and no matter how we try we cannot get warm.

I think of Nur and my father, and look up for al-Qutb, the star that never moves, before I remember we are under the cover of the shawls. I wish we could pull them down and wrap them around us, but if Akhtar thinks we are safer under a canopy we should do as he said.

I wonder if my father and brother are still alive under these same stars, but before I can summon their images I am asleep. We sleep until Akhtar comes back sometime in the middle of the night.

The little boys do not wake up, and I look out through the slits of my eyelids. Akhtar leads a donkey and carries a small bundle under his arm.

"Bread!" Khalida exclaims when Akhtar unwraps the bundle. "Where did you get it? And a donkey!"

"Never mind," Akhtar says softly. "We're very near the camp of the mujahideen, so we must move on. I wanted to find out what the bombing was about, and whether it would be safe to stay on this trail to Torkhum."

"And?" Khalida asks, her voice sounding angry again. "Was it worth risking your life and ours—"

"Listen," Akhtar says, cutting her off, "Pakistan has closed the border to refugees. We will have to stay at Torkhum. Walking there is very dangerous. American jets are destroying villages where they think Taliban are hiding, and bombing the areas where they travel. These are the same roads and pathways we've been traveling on. The smaller bombs are from the Taliban's grenade launchers. They're trying to stop deserters who are fleeing to Peshawar. We must leave the road and walk on our own through the hills. Anything else is too dangerous."

My heart begins to hammer again. Perhaps my father and Nur have escaped from the Taliban and I will find them in Peshawar! With the border closed, it will be difficult to get there, but somehow I will manage. For the first time I forget the gnawing in my stomach, and my eyes fly open.

"Get up, Najmah," Akhtar says when he sees I am awake. Khalida rouses her sons. "We must leave now and walk all night. We will sleep under cover during daylight."

Moon- and starlight guide us through the mountains, and I am able to keep our direction true by finding al-Qutb with the second knuckle of my fist, just as my father showed Nur and me what seems a lifetime ago in our village in Kunduz.

As we walk through the mountains, our feet slip over rocks and we have to hold on to each other to keep from falling off the trail and into the steep ravine on our downhill side. Intermittently clouds roll over the sky, obscuring the moon and the stars, and we walk with our hands on the boulders on the other side of the trail, some of which are the size of houses and hang precipitously over our heads.

The way is too steep and slippery to trust the animals to carry the children. Akhtar carries his older son, and Khalida and I take turns carrying the younger. We save our water, drinking it in little sips. There is nothing but rocks and dust in these hills, and long spaces to plummet into ravines. The bread is dry and tasteless, but we are so hungry we want to eat it all at once. Akhtar makes us take little bites, and the bread lasts many days—as long as the water.

We walk up a mountain until we feel our lungs

will burst. We walk through snow and rock, and I feel ice crystals between the soles of my feet and the soles of the sandals. I no longer feel my toes and fingers. Then we walk down the other side of the mountain, sliding and sometimes tumbling, struggling to stay together. Away from the mountaintop there is no snow—only rocks and boulders. As soon as we are down the other side there is another mountain before us. We eat snow, and slowly we eat our way through the stale, moldy bread the mujahideen have given Akhtar. We lose track of days. We do not sleep for many days and nights because Akhtar is afraid if we go to sleep we'll freeze to death.

When we come to rest one evening, we have nothing left to eat or drink. We are covered with dust, and I think if planes fly over us now we would be completely invisible. But we are at the foot of the last mountain and the air is not as icy, and so we will sleep this night.

It's been more than two weeks since I've last spoken, and I'm not certain I will ever be able to speak again. That night we sleep like the dead under the cover of an enormous boulder and our boulder-colored shawls.

NUSRAT
Peshawar, Pakistan

10

*T*hat night Nusrat lies on a wood-and-string cot in her garden. She is wrapped in a soft woolen shawl against the chill of the autumn night. She stares at the stars overhead. During the days she keeps busy with the class that meets under the persimmon tree. She doesn't have time to think whole thoughts about her husband. It's more as if he is infused in every thought she has about school or his family or her own or household matters. But at night she looks at the stars and imagines Faiz doing the same—perhaps now in a medical camp in Mazar-i-Sharif, to the north and west, about three hundred miles inside Afghanistan.

"I have tried to be angry with you," she says, looking at the stars, as if he can hear her through them. "I'd rather be angry than so terrified of what might happen to you. But it never works. You are the kindest man I know. You would never allow us to worry about you if you could help it." She is quiet, thinking how this simple fact is one of the reasons she's so frightened.

Every day that Nusrat goes to the bazaar, she hears news and rumors of fighting between the loose alliance of Afghan tribal warriors organized by the Americans and the Taliban, along with the Saudis and Africans and others who follow Osama bin Laden. The fighting has been fierce, and the number of deaths and injuries is mounting quickly. People are talking about the Americans dropping bombs on villages, killing innocent families. Nusrat lies still, trying not to think, and the memory of how she met Faiz plays inside her head like a movie on a screen.

Elaine Perrin loved everything about New York. Teaching middle school mathematics on the Upper West Side of Manhattan was challenging, and she loved her volunteer work at the animal shelter. Between her job and working on her master's degree at Columbia University, she barely had time to sleep and eat. Nobody knew her outside of school, and she loved the anonymity of the city. She missed her parents, but having grown up overprotected after Margaret's death she loved being on her own.

She loved her small apartment on Seventy-first Street near West End Avenue, just a block from the subway stop on Broadway, where the main bus routes stopped, too. The area had plenty of restaurants and shopping. The streets were crowded with students, women pushing baby carriages, people carrying musical instruments, people from every part of the world—men wearing turbans and long jackets, women wearing saris or robes that covered them head to foot. The air hummed with unfamiliar languages and mechanical noises. The sounds of life boiled around her like mist over the ocean.

Her building was a dilapidated brownstone that had once been a grand single-family house. It was close enough to walk to school, and Columbia was a short bus ride uptown. Her apartment was a studio, a fifth-floor walkup the size of her mother's kitchen. The halls and stairwell smelled of frying liver and canned peas. Elaine loved it.

She came back from teaching her last class and ate cottage cheese with a spoon out of the carton. She sat in the broad sill of the bay window, which looked out over the Hudson River. The sky over the water was gray and the wind had picked up so that it bent the tops of the trees at alarming angles. Leaves that had turned crisp and brown in the last dry throes of August blew down the street. Then rain spritzed against the windowpane. Elaine chucked the carton into the garbage and rinsed off her spoon before taking her raincoat and hat from the closet.

The buses slowed along Broadway in the rain and she thought it would be senseless to take an umbrella, which would turn inside out in the wind while she waited at the bus stop. She crossed to the window and shut it before turning off the lights and making sure her door was double-locked. She skipped down the stairway, sidestepping a bright yellow toy dump truck left by the small son of the people whose flat opened onto the landing two floors below hers. Rounding the last turn in the stairs, she bumped into someone who was running up the stairs as quickly as she was coming down.

He looked up with turquoise green eyes and a sharp intake of breath. "I'm sorry," he said, "I wasn't watching . . ."

"Neither was I," she said, smiling. "It was my fault." He nodded at her and kept going. He must be the person who'd moved into the rear fifth-floor apartment, she thought. He looked Middle Eastern, with a straight nose, fair skin, dark hair, and slim build.

Elaine had two courses at Columbia that term, and she spent evenings either in class or at the library. She had applied for her own carrel, but very few graduate students who were not doctoral candidates were able to get them. But the library staff had helped her to find a corner of a table where she could keep the reference materials she needed, and she had learned to tune out the activity around her.

It was raining even harder when Elaine came home that night, her raincoat plastered to her legs and her shoes soaking wet. The soles squeaked on the rubber stair treads, and water squished between her toes. She took the steps two at a time. She counted on the stairs for exercise—she didn't have time for the gym, although she managed a run in the park once or twice a week.

When she got to the fifth-floor landing, she thought she must have made a mistake counting and was only on four because the door to her apartment stood wide open. Peering inside, she saw her paisley cushions on the daybed, her carpet on the floor, her bedroom slippers where she'd left them inside the closet door, which never quite shut tightly.

She must have stood staring through the doorway for a few seconds before stepping inside. As she reached for the light switch, something bumped her hard in the chest, knocking her back against the doorframe. She looked up into two eyes that peered out from holes in a black woolen ski mask, just as the eyes' owner turned to jump down the full length of the top flight of steps.

"Hey!" Elaine shouted. "Stop! Stop him—he broke into my apartment," she yelled, bolting down the stairs after the man as he made the turn past the fourth-floor landing. A door opened on the landing of the third floor and a man came out. The masked guy hesitated for a second, then vaulted over the railing and dropped the remaining floors to the lobby below. He hit the floor rolling, and Elaine could see thick pads were sewn into the knees of his black overalls and the elbows of his red-and-black plaid jacket. A tool belt peeked out from underneath the jacket.

"Are you all right?" asked the father of the dump truck's owner.

"Yes! Call 911!" Elaine shouted and ran down the stairs as the thief grappled with the locked front door. Someone clattered down the stairs behind her, catching up with her between the third and second floors. Elaine could hear the thief still fumbling with the sticky lock on the heavy front door in the building's small vestibule.

"Are you crazy?" yelled the Middle Eastern man, holding on to her arm. "Let him go! What are you going to do if you catch him?" Elaine blinked. It was true. The thief could have a knife or a gun . . .

"What did he take?" asked the Middle Eastern man. Suddenly Elaine was completely out of breath, and she slumped back against the wall, feeling faint. She heard the door slam in the lobby downstairs as the thief escaped onto the street.

Elaine's neighbor put his arm around her upper back and supported her. "Come on," he said. "I'll help you to your apartment." The man on the third floor came back out to the landing with a cordless phone in his hand.

"The police will be here in just a minute," he said, calling up the stairwell after Elaine and her neighbor. "You want me to let them in?" The Middle Eastern man leaned over the banister.

"That would be very kind of you," he said. "I shall help her back upstairs. She's in 5A—would you mind sending them up?"

Elaine's stomach felt queasy and her head spun. Gratefully she leaned against the Middle Eastern man, and he helped her walk up the last flight to her door. "Please don't go," she said, her voice sounding weak.

"Go?" he said with a little laugh. "I couldn't

leave you in this condition. You're in shock. That is the only thing that could explain why you took off after a robber who might have been armed. You could have been killed." She looked at him more closely and saw that his turquoise green eyes sparkled. His lips turned up slightly at the corners.

He left the front door of her apartment open and helped her to sit on the daybed. He got a glass out and filled it from the water filter in her refrigerator. He handed it to her, and she took a sip.

"You're soaking wet," he said, pulling her hat from her head and removing her raincoat. Next he took off her shoes and peeled away her socks, then gently lifted her feet up onto the daybed. He tucked a blanket around her and brought a towel from the bathroom to dry her hair.

"I can't imagine what I was thinking," she said, still feeling dizzy. "Heaven only knows what would have happened if I'd caught up with him . . ."

"Sometimes adrenaline completely overpowers common sense," said her new neighbor. There was a commotion in the stairwell, which they could hear through the open doorway. Two policemen were climbing the last flight of steps to the fifth floor. One of them was red-faced and round-stomached. He was breathing hard as his partner knocked on the doorframe.

"Come in," Elaine called out, standing with the blanket around her shoulders and the towel in her hands. She introduced herself, and the police officers turned to her neighbor, who stepped forward and shook hands with them.

"I'm Dr. Faiz Ahmed Faiz," he said. "I live across the hall." Elaine recalled all that she could about the robber, with the chubby policeman writing as she spoke, occasionally asking her to repeat or clarify a detail.

"Anything missing?" asked the other officer, who was walking around the apartment, looking behind doors and into the bathroom, checking windows.

"My jewelry box is turned upside down," Elaine said, reaching to retrieve it from the floor beside her dresser. "But nothing seems to be gone. There wasn't much in it."

"He entered through the window," said the second policeman.

"But the door was open," she said.

"I can't explain that, but you need to get gates. All top-floor apartments in brownstones should have them. These guys can do three brownstones in a night from the roof. Gotta have gates." Elaine couldn't think of anything to say. She didn't want bars across her window. The view was what she loved most about her place. "You can get the kind that fold back in the daytime when you're at home," the officer said, as if reading her mind. "You won't even know you have them."

When they had gone, Dr. Faiz said he had to go to work.

"Are you all right?" he asked, peering closely at her. "Is there someone I can call to come and stay with you?" Elaine shook her head.

"I'll be okay," she said, smiling. "Thank you so much for helping me. What I did—or tried to do—was very stupid. Thank you." He grinned, and his smile showed remarkably even white teeth.

"I'm used to people who do things that aren't too smart," he said. "I work in an emergency room. You should eat something light and get some sleep. You'll be like brand-new in the morning." He had a slight accent and his eyes were animated. She liked his whole face.

The next day was Saturday, and with two hours free before she went to the library Elaine baked an apple spice cake. She crossed the hall to give it to Dr. Faiz, and when he didn't answer her knock, she brought it back to her apartment, feeling deflated. Just as she was closing her door, his opened and he peered out, blinking. His face was unshaven. He wore a white T-shirt, and she could see one striped pajama leg behind the half-opened door.

"I'm sorry," she said, "I didn't . . ."

"No problem," he said, waving his hand. "I need to get back to work." She held the cake out to him.

"I made this for you to say thank you," she said. His eyebrows shot up, and he took in a short, sharp breath in surprise.

"Please," he said, seeming almost at a loss for speech. "Just give me a few minutes to get dressed. Come back and I'll make us some tea and we'll have a piece of cake." When he greeted her fifteen minutes later, he was shaved and dressed in khaki trousers and a denim shirt with the sleeves rolled to the elbows. He looked as if he had slept a full twelve hours.

The moment Elaine entered his place, with its beautiful deep red carpets and large, hand-woven cushions on the floor, dark, carved tables that were low enough to eat from while seated on the cushions, old brass samovars, and embroidered wall hangings with mirrors sewn into them, she felt she was entering a world where she belonged.

On one table near the front door of Faiz's apartment sat the most exquisite book she'd ever seen, its covers of ancient, hand-tooled leather. She opened the book, and its pages were so thin you could see through them. They were inscribed in a graceful hand-drawn script in large gold and red and green letters and ornate borders. Faiz explained it was a Koran that was said to have been handed to his family by a follower of Muhammad hundreds of years ago.

A familiar feeling that her own life was insubstantial swept over Elaine as she ate the cake she'd brought and drank the sweet green tea flavored with cardamom that Faiz had offered. She wasn't thinking specifically of her mother's handmade chintz curtains, or the chenille spread on the bed she'd slept on since childhood, the plastic ivy tucked into the valance over the kitchen curtains, or the corduroy slipcovers on the sofa, or her father's vinyl recliner chair. But Elaine felt no connection to the world in which she grew up. Wearing her snow boots to Sunday school and carrying her patent leather Mary Jane shoes in a paper sack were just things she did. The details of her life—eating peanut butter and jelly sandwiches while sitting at the Formica kitchen counter after school, and drinking purple Kool-Aid on hot summer days—seemed to be the details of a faceless, nameless person. Nothing about her past life made her want to own it.

But in Faiz's apartment she felt a sense of having found something familiar and significant—a connection to a history and a way of life that she wanted to know more about and become more familiar with, as if it were a part of her own past that she'd almost forgotten.

In the half hour they spent together on that still-rainy Saturday before each of them went their separate ways to work, Elaine discovered that (1) Faiz was Persian—he had grown up in Afghanistan; (2) he was a physician at St. Luke's–Roosevelt Hospital; (3) love at first sight was not the ridiculous romantic notion she'd always thought it to be.

11

When we awake late that afternoon, I do not feel hungry for the first time in many days. But I am so tired and weak I can barely move. All I want is more sleep.

"We're very close to Torkhum," Akhtar says, shaking my shoulder. "If you can walk for just two hours more, we'll be there." It seems to take forever to get my feet under me and rise to a standing position, even with Khalida pulling on my hands. I cannot feel my feet, although they are bloody with broken blisters, torn nails, and cracked calluses from walking so long in the rigid, rough sandals. Akhtar and Khalida carry the boys for fear they're too weak to hold on to the donkey's harness.

"Just over the next hill," Akhtar keeps saying to urge Khalida and me on. "We can make it." I don't believe him, but the sun is still above the horizon when we see the dust and hear the noise of the border-crossing town of Torkhum. A group of people stand in a clearing among rows of tents, where a large truck is parked. The truck is not brightly painted like the ones that ply the roads of Afghanistan, with portraits of warriors and mountain scenes and springing tigers. It is a plain white truck with the Red Crescent insignia painted on the doors and across the front and back.

Workers surround the truck, rolling its canvas cover back to expose what is inside. Some of the workers look like Afghans, while others are foreigners with pale eyes and skin. One of the foreigners stands at the back of the truck and begins to fill spouted metal jars of water from a tank.

Standing beside the foreign workers is an Afghan man with a board that has paper clipped to it. When he sees us, he motions for us to get in the line formed by the people who arrived by road just minutes ahead of us, who look like refugees, too. There are ten or so family groups, each made up of three or four or five children, one or two women, and one or two elders.

Their clothes are tattered, and like us they are covered with dust.

"Ah-salaam-aleikum," says the man with the papers, greeting the entire group. "I am Tarek Ahmed, malek of this refugee station at Torkhum. You're in luck." He turns back toward the truck. "We've been three days without supplies and this truck arrived just two hours ago." The malek speaks Dari, which is our language, although it sounds different.

The refugees stand quietly, their eyes blank with hunger as the pale-haired volunteers count out bright yellow packets stamped with words written in a foreign language in black ink. The packets are about the size of my forearm from my wrist to my elbow.

The malek asks the man at the head of each group questions and writes their answers on the paper clipped to his board. When he finishes with his questions, a foreign woman with white hair hands over one yellow packet for each family member. We are the last family group in the line, and I worry they will run out of yellow packets before we get to the truck.

As we stand waiting I notice that a woman in the group ahead of us holds a bundle of rags close to her chest, and I think of the women who begged beside the road in the last city we passed through, where we filled our water pots at the well. When the malek finishes asking his questions of the old man at the head of the group, he asks to look inside the woman's bundle. She clutches the rags close to her chest and refuses to show him. An older woman who arrived with her speaks gently to her and pries the bundle from her arms.

The older woman pulls aside the rags to reveal the pale face of a new infant, its surmeh-rimmed eyes shut and its mouth a thin blue line. It is still as a stone and I know it is dead. The older woman hands the bundle over to the malek, who looks at the small white face, then pulls the corner of the top rag, which is a tattered shawl, back over it. He hands the bundle back to the older woman and wordlessly writes something on his paper.

Then it is our turn. The malek asks Akhtar where we have come from, what our names are, and how we are related. Akhtar points to Khalida and the two boys and says they are his wife and youngest children. As he speaks, Khalida pulls the turban from her head and in the same movement drapes it around her face like a veil.

"Why is your wife dressed like a boy?" the malek asks.

"If something happened to me she would be safer if it was not known she was a woman," Akhtar says quietly.

"But she might have been taken and made to fight," says the malek. I think of Nur and know he's right.

Akhtar shrugs. "That would be the better evil," he says, resting his hand on my shoulder. "This," he says, "is Shaheed, my oldest son." The malek looks at me for a moment.

"How long have you been walking?" the malek asks me.

"Shaheed cannot speak," Akhtar says. Then the malek wants to know how Akhtar has escaped being taken away by the Taliban.

"I am mujahid with the Harakat-i-Kunduz," Akhtar replies. "I led my family up into the hills before the Taliban came to our village. We did not travel on the road." The malek looks at each of us as if examining us to determine whether Akhtar is telling the truth.

"The trip was difficult and dangerous," Akhtar says, "but I have experience in the mountains. The Taliban would have killed my family and me if they had found us. I would like to leave my family here where they will be safe, and return to fight against the Taliban." The malek nods at Akhtar, who is the only grown and able-bodied man in the group of refugees that have arrived this same day.

"Get your family settled first," says the malek, and then he turns to help the volunteers secure the canvas over the yellow packets of food that remain in the back of the truck.

We tear open our yellow packets without moving from the spot where we stood when the foreigner handed them to Akhtar. Inside are dried fruit bars, a brown paste, and flat, grayish-white disks the size of a tin of snuff. They look like nothing edible I've ever seen.

"Eat them slowly," the malek says. "They're protein wafers. They don't taste very good, but they will make you strong. Drink water with them. You must make them last, as we don't know when we'll get more."

I am so disappointed I want to cry. Khalida's face turns red, and she blinks her eyes as if to keep back tears. Even Akhtar presses the biscuits between his fingers and sniffs at them as if he cannot imagine swallowing them. But we have been so long without food we know we have no choice, and we sit in the middle of the road behind the Red Crescent truck and nibble at the contents of the packets, which we wash down with sips of warm, metallic-tasting water.

The little boys cry with frustration, and Khalida and Akhtar break off bits of the biscuits in their fingers and place them on their sons' tongues. The smaller boy spits it out and shakes his head to keep his mother from putting more into his mouth.

My first bite has no taste. It is brittle and crumbles on my tongue like a piece of mountain shale. I manage to swallow the biscuit with water so I don't have to taste very much of it. And after a few minutes my stomach doesn't feel so hollow and weak and the feeling begins to return to my arms and legs. I manage to eat another biscuit in the same way, and a little while afterward my body begins to regain feeling that I hadn't realized I'd lost.

After we eat, Akhtar leads us to a clearing beyond the tents where the malek has directed him. Khalida and the boys and I wrap up in our shawls and huddle together to sleep. Akhtar goes off to see about finding more quilts and a tent. Without the ache of hunger in our stomachs we sleep immediately and deeply, although we have not been awake for more than a few hours.

I awake with a start sometime in the middle of the night. The air is still and cold and the stars shine brightly overhead. The camel kneels near us, chewing softly and shifting her position from time to time. I hear snoring from groups of people who lie nearby and the shuffling of the donkeys tethered together near the mud-brick house where the malek stays.

Suddenly the last words Akhtar spoke before we slept play through my head. "If my family is to stay here they'll need shelter," he had said to the malek.

I have no intention of staying in Torkhum. Without my realizing it, the entire time we've been on the way from Kunduz to the Pakistani border, a plan has been forming in my head. I am barely able to keep from jumping up and running off into the night. But I know I cannot travel alone to Peshawar to look for my father and brother. The border is closed, and I don't even know which way to go. I am unwilling to set off again with no food. And so I lie awake the rest of the night thinking about my plan, staring at the stars, and praying for guidance.

12

Nusrat rises before the sun and wraps a shawl around her shoulders. She goes to the kitchen in her bedroom slippers and fills the kettle from the hand pump in the sink. She strikes a match and holds it to the kerosene stove until the blue flame pops to life. She lays out the things for tea while the water heats, and when she hears the tickle of bubbles rising to the surface inside the kettle, she carries it to the bathroom. She mixes it with cold water that Husna drew the night before to make a warm bath in the large plastic tub and rinse water in the bucket.

As she pours, the hot water sends clouds of

steam into the chilly morning air. Standing on a wooden pallet over the open drain in the cement floor, she pours the water over herself with a ladle. The water stings her face and arms and causes gooseflesh to rise all over her body. She rubs a bar of rough, tallowy homemade soap over her skin quickly, then rinses and steps into the tub to get warm for a few minutes before rubbing herself briskly with a rough, sun-dried towel. Nusrat loves the austerity of heating her own water and bathing in the cold. It makes her feel alive to live so simply.

When she has dressed, she pulls up her shawl to cover her hair and faces the qibla, a small circle she's pinned to the curtain of her bed-sitting room to indicate the direction of Mecca.

"Bismillah ar-Rahman ar-Raheem," she begins, "in the name of God, the compassionate, the merciful." She never misses her prayers. They remind her of the choices she has made, how they have brought her here, and propelled her toward making a difference in the world. They remind her she would not prefer to be anyone else or to live anywhere else. And they connect her directly to Faiz, who is saying his prayers at the same moment somewhere, perhaps fifty mountains away.

Nusrat converted to Islam before she and Faiz even discussed marriage. She decided on her own, without telling Faiz of her decision. The idea struck her the first time she entered Faiz's apartment in New York, the day she brought the apple spice cake to thank him for helping her after her apartment was broken into.

After her sister's death Elaine began a quest for meaning. She could not accept that the God of her childhood would take her little sister. Elaine longed for a poetic and mysterious sense of order that would explain where Margaret had gone and why she had gone there. She held out hope for finding her answers in church. But she could never quite see past the wheezing of the old organ, the self-conscious reading of Scriptures, sermons that caused her to wriggle in her seat, and summer Bible School lessons that inspired her to sit under the table and eat paste.

Her search led her to a disabled neighbor who told biblical stories from her wheelchair, illustrating them with cloth figures she moved around on a felt board. After a time Elaine wondered what these stories had to do with her.

She had serious questions about God and the chaos she found around her. Did God have a plan? How did Margaret's death fit into this scheme, and how could Elaine find her place in it? The adults in her world were unable to answer her questions and unwilling to discuss them. "You must have faith," they said. But no one could tell her where to look for faith. Her mother washed her mouth out with soap once after Sunday school when she'd ventured to say that if Jesus had tried to walk on the sea He would have gotten wet. Eventually she stopped asking questions, but they continued in her head despite every effort to switch them off.

For years Elaine prayed for some small sign that would set her mind at ease. If God would send her a small signal—one that only she would recognize— she vowed to believe without questioning. She looked everywhere: in the rainbow-colored scales of fish and the dew on the grass on summer mornings, in the shapes of snowflakes.

Her first inkling of the significance she longed for came in college, when she read about the Fibonacci sequence. Its expression in the precision of the spirals of seashells, the symmetry of the fronds of ferns, the branches of trees, and the petals of flowers was something she could hold on to, and she decided to study math in college.

Until Elaine met Faiz, all that she knew of Islam was what she'd read—that it was a warlike religion with many followers who hated Christians and wanted a return to a past in which women must be hidden away. Then, opening the Koran on Faiz's table that Saturday morning, she felt a surge of energy leap to her fingertips like an electrical shock. She had to subject Islam to the same rigors she'd put her own religion through.

"How does a compassionate man like you—a doctor who helps people—reconcile himself to a faith that thinks so poorly of women?" Elaine asked Faiz one evening.

"Faith is only between each person and God," he had answered quietly. "If anything, the Koran would judge women to be superior because they're more caring and more honest. Here the news from the Middle East and Afghanistan tells only about Islamic fundamentalist fanatics, and so I think non-Muslims don't believe me at all when I say such things."

As she grew to know Faiz, Elaine saw that he seemed entirely without ego and spoke in the most respectful and loving tones about his mother and sister. He was awed by Elaine's knowledge of mathematics and the heavens and the creation of the universe. He encouraged her to continue her studies to earn a Ph.D. in physics, which she hoped to do one day.

Elaine stopped wanting so much for God to reveal Himself as the composer of the world's infinite complexities. What she longed for was the kind of peace and assurance that radiated from Faiz. It was one of the things that drew her so powerfully to him.

"At least tell me what you think 'faith' is," she said to Faiz one afternoon when they were listening to music in his apartment. Faiz raised his hands, palms upward, and smiled.

"This is faith—you don't think such a wondrous thing as music can be created by a human being alone, do you?" Elaine regarded him carefully.

"Well then, what's the difference between your faith and a Christian's faith?" Elaine asked. "Christians and Muslims alike write music and poetry and paint and draw."

"Really faith is the same for everyone. For me it's a simple matter of having grown up knowing and following the teachings of Islam. What the Koran teaches about how people should live their lives isn't very different from the laws of Christianity or Judaism or Hinduism."

To find out precisely what the Koran said, Elaine consulted the Imam Inayatollah of the mosque on the Upper West Side of Manhattan.

"I am a mathematician," she said. "I need a religion that's compatible with science and mathematics. In Islam, is there a belief in an order to the universe?"

"Islam is the cradle of modern mathematics and astronomy," the imam said. "As a mathematician you must have read of the Central Asian astronomer al-Khwarizmi?" She said she had not. "He wrote the theory that led Fibonacci to his famous number sequence. Al-Khwarizmi was a Muslim." He told her about Omar Khayyam, the eleventh-century Persian poet, astronomer, and philosopher who made observations on algebra that were the foundation of the study of mathematics for the next five hundred years.

"Does it take a very long time to complete studies to become a Muslim?" she asked. His answer surprised her.

"It is very simple," said the imam. "To convert to Islam it is necessary only to proclaim that there is one God and one Prophet, Muhammad," he said. "After that, matters are between you and God. If you decide to act in accordance with your conscience and these simple laws, then you are a Muslim."

Elaine took a course in Arabic at Columbia so she could read the Koran for herself. And before long she had learned to savor the taste of the words on her tongue.

On evenings when she didn't work at the animal shelter she studied Islam at the masjid. It wasn't only the words of the imam and the teachings of the Koran that convinced her that moderation, peace, and hope were more characteristic of Islam than the warlike stereotypes she was familiar with. It was also the people she met there, who treated her and each other with respect, courtesy, and kindness. She looked up

Islamic teachings on the Internet and saw answers to her questions about her own life scroll down before her eyes as if they were written to her in a letter.

What moved her most were references in the Koran to the creation of the universe from smoke in one great cosmic event that gave birth to all matter; to the ever-expanding nature of the universe; and stars that "pierce the universe" like black holes. All of these references were made more than a thousand years before science knew about them.

Elaine did not find the answers to her questions about why Margaret had died and where she had gone. It was enough to find a sense of order in the universe, and to believe that Margaret was somehow still in it. Elaine no longer had to know precisely where her sister was.

Walking through Central Park, holding hands and eating ice cream, Elaine and Faiz had long discussions about the Koran.

"Must all Muslims be given Islamic names?" Elaine asked him one evening when they both had a couple of hours away from work to spend together.

"It isn't necessary," Faiz answered, "but it's a good thing. Islamic names are meaningful as ideals—for example, my name means 'victorious.' The idea is a little like achieving goodness by association. Your name also identifies you as a Muslim."

"What would my Islamic name be?" Elaine asked. Faiz looked at her a second longer.

"Nusrat," he said finally, stopping and turning to face her. "Nusrat means 'help' or 'one who helps.' You help people and you help animals. That would be a good name for you." And so he began to call her Nusrat. Not long afterward Nusrat and Faiz had gone to the imam at the mosque and Nusrat pronounced the Shahada: "There is one God and Muhammad is the messenger of God." The imam smiled at her and said, "Be a good Muslim." Her conversion had been simple, but it had changed her life.

Nusrat hears Husna moving about the kitchen, relighting the stove and filling the kettle with water for tea. After she and Faiz married, he made tea each morning, bringing her a cup in bed to awaken her in his beautiful New York apartment before leaving for work at the hospital. Sadness wafts over Nusrat like a chilly breeze that makes her draw her shawl more tightly around her. She cannot think how she will manage to find her way through another day, teaching the children, telephoning or visiting her mother-in-law and Asma, shopping in the bazaar, helping Husna with the housework, and facing again the arrival of no letter from Faiz. How will she find the power to do it?

With Faiz gone, she feels as if one of her main parts is missing, causing her nerves to misfire and her intent to falter. It takes all of her will to extend her hand slowly toward the bed where she has laid her nightclothes. But she gathers them up and her hand begins to move of its own will again as she puts them away in the cupboard and draws the curtains back from her window. A row of small gray birds sits on the top of the wall outside, and she feels better.

When Husna has brought her tea on a tray with a woolen cozy over the small porcelain pot, Nusrat sits down at the small wooden desk in her bedroom and writes a note to Faiz. The husband of one of Husna's friends, a maid for Dr. Naveed, who lives down the street, is traveling to Bamiyan. Nusrat sends notes to Faiz with everyone she hears of who heads into the North of Afghanistan. No one refuses her, for everyone caught up in the war has relatives waiting for word of them in the refugee camps. Everyone understands.

A week earlier Nusrat sent a note with a group of mujahideen who were traveling to Baghlan, to the south of Kunduz. She had even sent a note with a grape seller to Faizabad, far to the east of Mazar-i-Sharif, in the hope it would find its way to her husband.

She refuses to wonder why no notes have come

back. She knows many of her notes have not reached him for a variety of reasons. Her couriers couldn't find Faiz in one place and so handed the note to someone traveling to another city where he might be.

She has heard rumors, but none of them can be confirmed. One rumor was that the Taliban had forced a foreign doctor in Bamiyan to go with them to treat their injured fighters. Another was that the Americans had accidentally dropped a bomb on an emergency clinic and that everyone in the clinic had died. Each story wounded Nusrat like the blade of a sword, but there was no way for her to find out whether what she heard was true. They couldn't all be true, she reasoned. Until she heard something credible to the contrary, she would not believe any of them.

"My dearest husband," Nusrat writes. "Greeting you this way makes you real again to me, for without word of you I begin to doubt you ever existed." She stops writing. Faiz and his family regard pessimism as weakness. She tears the sheet from her writing tablet and wads it into a ball. She begins again. "My dearest husband: This morning as I said my prayers I asked Allah—as I do every morning—to return you safely to me. Today I feel that He will. I have a feeling today is a day of good luck!" She tells him about sitting with Jamshed and Sultan and watching the meteor shower in her garden. She doesn't tell him about the explosion in the bazaar.

When she has finished, she folds the note and puts it into an envelope, sealing it with wax and the impression of Faiz's gold ring, which she wears on the index finger of her right hand. On the front she writes: "Dr. Faiz Ahmed Faiz, Surgeon, Medical Clinic, Mazar-i-Sharif." She calls Husna and asks her to take the note to Dr. Naveed's house. Husna hesitates for a moment.

"Go on," Nusrat says. "I'll get my own breakfast and make milk-tea for the children. I don't want to miss the man who is going to Bamiyan." Without saying a word, Husna takes the envelope and turns away.

Not long afterward that same morning there is word from the North of Afghanistan. Haroon, the malek of the Shahnawaz refugee camp, rings the bell outside Nusrat's blue gate. The bell jangles noisily until Husna can cross the courtyard from the kitchen door at the back of the house. Nusrat comes close behind Husna to see what the commotion is about.

In his excitement Haroon—who normally is polite and reserved—pushes past Husna and speaks to Nusrat. The morning is still chilly and gray, with a fine mist hovering along the top of the garden wall.

"Kunduz is liberated!" says Haroon, forgetting

to even greet Nusrat and Husna, blurting it out and waving his arms. Nusrat has never seen him so animated. "The Taliban are gone. The border has reopened and men are coming to Peshawar from all over the North of Afghanistan to collect their families. Soon they will return to their farms and grazing lands and life will be as it was. Allah be praised!"

Nusrat's heart lurches wildly inside her chest. If Kunduz is free from the Taliban, perhaps soon Mazar-i-Sharif will be, too. Faiz might even come sooner than she had hoped! She thinks of the note she wrote in the morning, and realizes that she—like her in-laws and all Afghans—has begun to think of the future in terms of omens.

Instead of sitting down to breakfast and her morning newspaper, Nusrat bakes Welsh cakes, using tiny sweet sulaiman raisins from the bazaar, and sugar, and refined flour. It's her mother's recipe, and she thinks of other family celebrations. She hums as she works, the dust of white flour hanging cheerfully in the air. Husna stays out of her way, sweeping in the living room, then coming back to check whether she's needed.

When the children arrive at Nusrat's blue gate, she greets them as usual, standing inside the back garden. But this morning she insists that the mothers come inside for tea. "It's chilly, and tea will warm you," she says to each mother, holding on to her arm. "I have made special cakes to break your fast. Kunduz is liberated! It's a special day."

When everyone has arrived, she beckons to Husna and asks her to bring the tea and Welsh cakes out into the garden, where the mothers and children sit on the cots drawn into the shape of a U under the persimmon tree.

Mansoora and Amina are the last to arrive. With the food Nusrat gives them and ration cards from the United Nations, they have both lost the frightened, haunted look they wore when they'd first come to the Persimmon Tree School. Mansoora's hands are clean and her eyes have life in them again.

"Have you heard?" Mansoora asks when they're seated. "The Taliban are gone!"

13

I must have dozed around dawn because the last thing I remember is the sky turning a pale green and gold at the horizon. The next thing I know, there is shouting and jostling and the air is mixed with dust. A wagonload of apples has arrived from across the border, and the crowd, which had been quiet and orderly the night before, clamors and elbows until the fruit is gone.

We sleep two more nights under the stars, and during the day milk and ghee and lentils from Pakistan are handed out in addition to the fruit bars and gray biscuits. Slowly we begin to recover our strength.

On our fourth day in the camp at Torkhum, the malek comes around and asks Akhtar and the men who arrived the same day we did to come with him. People from the United Nations are giving out tents and more food. By that evening Akhtar and Khalida have a dark greenish-brown tent and the small piece of land on which it sits to call home.

But I am not inclined to call any place home, except for the farm where I've always lived with my father and mother and brother in the Kunduz Hills, below the rim of Koh-i-Dil. Although the house no longer stands, I know I must find my father and brother and return there with them. My father asked my mother to stay and keep the property safe from Uncle and the Taliban, and I intend to do exactly what he asked her to do. But first I must find them, and the place to look is Peshawar, across the border in Pakistan. Peshawar has been the city of Afghan people running from war for as long as I can remember. I don't know how I will get there, but get there I must.

I wander about the bazaar and the refugee camp at Torkhum. Every day more tents spring up, and the lanes between them seem alive with children, who run in packs like wild dogs, shrieking and laughing and playing. Everyone in the camp has to take turns filling basins for bathing and laundry at a standing water pipe near the malek's house. Our turn comes only every third day.

Khalida spends entire days waiting in lines—first for drinking water, which we still get from the volunteers at the place where we collect our food, and then again for whatever food has arrived from Peshawar. Trucks arrive filled with clothing—some of it from foreign countries, mounds of strange shoes with pointed toes and very tall heels, and Western-style shirts and trousers and, best of all, warm sweaters. We stand in line for clothes, too.

I am given a brand-new Punjabi dereshi made out of a lightweight woolen fabric. It's warm and clean and too large. I roll the trouser legs to keep them from trailing in the dirt and the sleeves to leave my hands free to haul water.

The women stay mostly inside the tents, and only close neighbors visit back and forth, sitting under the open canvas flaps. I take advantage of being dressed as a boy to wander in the makeshift bazaar that has sprung up at the edge of the tent village, with vendors of fruits and vegetables, used clothing, soap, mirrors, plastic basins, and paper. In one part of the bazaar children wearing torn and dirty clothing squat on the ground calling out odd bits for sale: plastic bags, empty metal cans—or just the lids—and shoes they've taken from the feet of dead people. Several shops that sell shoes have signs over their open doorways that say *One Shoe*. They sell single shoes to the survivors of mines that are planted in the roads and the mountain passes of Afghanistan.

My feet have healed, and the sandals offer some protection from the cold. I help the malek by filling water jars so that he might favor us when food is available. The malek has come to rely on Akhtar for his physical strength and good judgment and on me for my willingness to do whatever job presents itself. I think how much the malek will miss Akhtar after he leaves to rejoin the mujahideen.

Khalida never puts her turban back on after that first day, and her short-cropped hair has just begun to grow over the tops of her ears. She wears a bright blue dereshi that came from one of the Red Crescent trucks. She covers her head with a chadr when she goes out to stand in line for water or food, and seems to be more comfortable dressed as a woman again. She does not like my comings and goings and tries to keep me in the tent with her to help with the little boys and the cooking. But Akhtar stands up for me.

"This is not the girl Najmah," he whispers one morning when the five of us are closed up inside the tent. "For the time being, she's more useful as the boy Shaheed. If he stays indoors and helps you with the children all the time as you'd like, everyone will know he's a girl."

I think about Akhtar's words. He is right. I am no longer the girl Najmah of Golestan, that child who was afraid of leopards. I am afraid of nothing after what I've seen. Neither am I a boy named Shaheed. But I must pretend to be Shaheed if I am to look for my father and brother in Peshawar. I do not care how I appear to others. Reuniting with them is my one and only reason for existence, and if I must do it as Shaheed, then I will be Shaheed for as long as necessary.

I have proved very adept at finding food when there seems to be none, and so Khalida reluctantly agrees to let me have my freedom for now.

For all of her kindness toward me, I have begun to resent Khalida. It isn't only that she tries to make me stay in the tent and help with her work, or even that she disapproves of my acting like a boy. It's more that she has her family, every one of them, safe around her. And I have no one.

I still have not spoken since the day I took the animals up into the hills before my mother and Habib were killed. But it is not because I am afraid. As I gain strength and my resolve grows to leave for Peshawar, I begin to think I might be able to talk again if I want to. A plan begins to grow within me to return to Kunduz and resume life on our farm. It will be very sad without my mother and Habib. But if I cannot find Baba-jan and Nur in Peshawar, I will wait for them in Kunduz, where I am prepared to fight for what belongs to my family. This plan fires my heart, and I begin to believe I can do almost anything I want to do.

I feel I must keep my distance from Khalida and Akhtar because I know I will leave them soon. If Akhtar leaves first, I am afraid I will have to stay and help Khalida. And so I keep my silence as well as my distance. And I watch very carefully for the chance to leave first.

By the seventh day in the refugee camp at Torkhum I know I am strong enough to reach Peshawar. It is a day's walk, perhaps more, but I do not intend to walk. At least twice a day a truck comes from the Pakistani border city loaded with food or clothing. Workers divide the cargo among the refugees from the backs of the trucks, and the malek pays the driver. The truck then turns around and drives back down the road toward Peshawar.

Then on the eighth day five trucks come, and there seem to be more on the way. The number of refugees also has grown since the border closed, with the tent village occupying two times as much space as it did a week earlier.

I don't dare ask if anyone from the trucks will take me to Peshawar. I know Akhtar will hear of it and will keep me from going. I have to watch for an opportunity without appearing to be watching.

My chance comes on our twelfth night at Torkhum. By then the camps are in confusion because word has come that the mujahideen have driven the Taliban out of Kunduz and other areas of the North. People say the Americans will rebuild houses and towns. Pakistan has reopened the border, and everyone waits for husbands and brothers and fathers to come to the refugee settlements and take their families home. Less attention is paid to the trucks, and my chances for getting to Peshawar improve even as I wonder if I should go back to Kunduz instead.

A truck filled with pears arrives from Peshawar just an hour before the sun sets. I am filling two-liter jars with water from a large metal tank on the back of a wooden cart and placing them on a table where the volunteer on duty hands them out to refugees, who have been arriving all day in a steady stream. The driver of the truck calls to the volunteer, a young woman with fair skin and red hair pulled back in a tail that hangs down her back.

"Unload them," the driver says to her in Dari.

"I can't do," she says.

"Now! Do it now!" the driver shouts. The young woman turns her hands palm up in a gesture of helplessness. I know the volunteers speak little Dari, and I don't speak her language. This public disrespect is so unusual that I put down the jar I carry and stand by to see what will happen next. At that moment the malek comes out of his house, pulling his shawl around his shoulders against the chilly early evening air.

"What is it?" he asks the driver of the truck.

"This cow won't unload the fruit so I can get back to Peshawar," says the driver, swinging down from his seat in the brightly painted cab of the lorry. He is a rough man with an unkempt beard that's clumped together from lack of washing. He wears a dirty dereshi, and his feet are bare, although it is very cold.

"She's not supposed to unload fruit," the malek says. "If we unload these pears, they'll disappear in two minutes. And it won't be the refugees who get them."

"That's your problem," says the driver, drawing on a clove-scented cigarette. "I have to get back to Peshawar tonight."

"You can't drive this road at night," the malek says. "The Pakistani Army will stop you if you're lucky. Or bandits will kill you and steal your truck. One or the other—I guarantee it." The truck driver spits at the malek's feet.

"I'll take the pears back and sell them in Peshawar," the driver says.

"You're crazy!" says the malek. "You've wasted a trip. I won't pay you and you're risking your life!"

I hesitate only a moment to consider the malek's prediction. This is the first chance I've seen for a ride to Peshawar, and I know Akhtar is anxious to rejoin the mujahideen to help them rout the Taliban from the rest of the country. Once he leaves, Khalida will keep close watch over me. I don't want to risk being caught by bandits or the Pakistani Army. But I am on my own now, and I decide to take my chances instead of waiting until it might be too late.

I back away from where the malek and the truck driver argue, and move toward an opening in the canvas tied over the fruit at the back of the truck. I try to stick my head inside, but the load is packed too tightly and there is no room. I begin to look for a way in from the top of the truck.

Overhanging the road are the branches of a huge neem tree. One branch sits just inches above the top of the canvas, which stretches tightly over a frame to form the roof and sides of a cover for the cargo. I move to the trunk of the tree and grab a low-hanging branch and swing my leg up to crook a foot, then a knee over the limb. I pull myself up so that my belly lies across it. At that instant the truck engine starts with a cough.

"Stop!" the malek shouts. "I can't let you leave."

The truck driver laughs, shouts obscenities out the window, and puts the truck into gear. It begins to roll backward. I think, "I'll never make it." But I hear the truck door open again, and the truck lurches to a stop after rolling just a few inches. So I keep climbing. I stand on the lower limb and reach up to a higher one that will lead me to the branch that now almost brushes the canvas covering the fruit.

The malek and the truck driver shout at each other some more, and I lower myself from the branch onto the canvas and drop to my stomach. I crawl on my elbows and knees toward the back of the truck and look under the canvas. There is barely room between the pile of pears and the cover, but I am afraid that if I try to ride outside I'll be discovered, or worse, I'll fall off when the truck gathers speed or careens around the sharp bends in the road.

I loosen the rope laced across the opening in the canvas and press my head and shoulders through. It feels as if several minutes pass while I squirm, kicking my feet to propel me forward. Once I'm inside, my breath comes in panicked gasps, but I don't dare rest.

I reach outside with shaking fingers and retie the rope in a knot so no one will suspect that I have added myself to the load of pears.

It doesn't make any sense at all for the driver to take his load back to Peshawar. Perhaps he is really a smuggler, I think. But I cannot wait for another truck. This may be my only chance to find Baba-jan and Nur, so I stay inside, lying on top of the fruit. I no longer hear what goes on between the driver and the malek. Eventually the truck starts to move again.

The truck jounces and jolts along a road that is so rough it feels as if it's been bombed. The fruit is cold and lumpy and hard beneath me, and I am worried the whole time that if the Pakistani Army catches me they'll send me to jail. Or worse, bandits might stop the truck and steal the fruit and kill me. It occurs to me that the driver is lying and that the truck may go somewhere other than Peshawar. Even if it does go to Peshawar, I have no idea how I will get away without the driver discovering me. He is mean and more than a little crazy, and I am afraid of him. I remind myself that I had little choice and I hope that Allah will protect me.

We are not far along the road that leads from Torkhum to Peshawar when the truck comes to a sudden stop, shifting the load forward and jamming my head against one of the metal rods that serve as a skeleton for the canvas tarpaulin. It has begun to rain, gently at first, but then the water drums steadily on the canvas. This is the first rain in many years, and I've almost forgotten the sound. Again I hear angry voices outside, although I cannot hear what is said because of the rain. I wiggle my way forward to an opening in the canvas above the cab of the truck and peek out over the driver's side.

I wish I hadn't looked. Three men stand with rifles pointing at where the driver sits high in the cab. Bandits, I think, all of them as rough and mean-looking as the driver. They order him to get out of the cab. He shouts something back at them, but I can't hear what he says. The rain falls harder. The light is dim and fading. The rain plasters the men's clothing against their bodies and legs, and the ends of their turbans hang limply.

I consider jumping to the ground and running. Boulders line the road, and beyond them on the driver's side the mountain drops off steeply into what looks like an abyss. I scoot over a little and look out over the passenger side, where another gunman stands with his rifle aimed at the cab. The hill that rises above that shoulder of the road is rocky and seems to be made of loose dirt that has turned to mud and has begun to slide down over the boulders in gooey masses. It would be very difficult to escape in either direction. Better to stay where I am and hope I won't be discovered until the truck stops at its destination—and that the destination is Peshawar!

Then I hear a gunshot, and my heart hammers so loudly I'm afraid the men will discover me in my hiding place. The truck rocks beneath me as if several people are climbing into the cab. I look out over the driver's side again in time to see the driver being thrown out the door just as the truck begins to move forward again. He lies facedown in the mud as the truck rolls forward, and he does not move. As the truck gathers speed, I think how short the distance is between life and death.

My breath comes in large ragged gulps. I try to tell myself to keep calm and crawl to the back opening of the canvas. By then the truck is going too fast for me to jump off. It slides and swerves, sloshing through muddy ruts, but it never slows, and I fear we will miss a turn and plunge down into the ravine. Small rocks from the sliding hill of mud on the other side of the road patter onto the canvas over my head. I pray none of the overhanging boulders comes loose to squash us flat. I pray the truck is still headed for Peshawar. If the pears are being stolen to be sold, Peshawar is the most logical destination. I also pray that the bandits won't unload the fruit before I can get away.

NAJMAH
Near Peshawar, Pakistan

14

I feel as if I've been tossed and bruised in the back of this fruit truck for hours. In reality, we've been on the road again for only a short time. But it's plenty of time for me to think about what I have done, and how it will end up. It seems far more likely that I will be killed than arrive safely in Peshawar. And if I arrive safely, how will I get away from these dangerous men? I will need a lot of luck. I've never thought about luck before, and now I consider that my luck has not been good these last weeks. But I cannot let myself be immobilized by fear.

Without warning, the truck slows and turns. If

the ride seemed bumpy before, now I fear that the vehicle will break down altogether as we seem to lurch from the one boulder to another. After a few minutes of this, the truck stops. I can't hear the men inside the cab, nor can I feel any movement. Perhaps they've turned off the road because they decided the rain made it too dangerous to continue. Perhaps they are asleep.

I think at first of jumping to the ground and taking my chances with traveling on foot by myself. I think of the malek's words about how dangerous it is to travel in this area. And I think of the murder of the driver, and I cannot make myself decide what to do. As I lie on the pears, I think that this rain is a sign that Allah is returning the earth to us. With the Taliban defeated in the North, we have a chance to rebuild our house and to live in peace again. If this is a sign from Allah, perhaps it also is a sign that He is looking after me. With this thought, I realize how exhausted I am and I fall into a deep sleep.

Sometime around dawn the doors of the truck open and slam closed again. I am instantly alert. The motor roars to life and the truck lurches over the boulders again as it turns in a circle. The rain has stopped. I lift the canvas. The truck pulls onto the roadway and we continue our journey.

The truck slows about the time that light begins

to filter through the canvas. Eventually we come to a stop. The truck moves backward and forward a couple of times before the driver switches off the engine. I pull aside the canvas a tiny bit to see that we are parked alongside a large bazaar. The rain has slowed to a drizzle, and I hear people and vehicles moving through the mud.

Straight ahead is a lane of shops where workers prepare skewers of meat and pots of tea for customers to eat at rough tables with wooden benches drawn up to them. The tables and cots are empty at this hour, and my stomach is queasy at the thought of food after lying so long atop the fruit in the truck and wondering how I will get out without being caught.

Beside the lane with the food stalls is another alley covered with cloths strung over poles high overhead. I cannot see what these shops sell under their tarpaulins, but I think I might try to hide there. I move cautiously toward the back of the truck and peer through the parting of the canvas. Several men stand behind the truck. Four of them are the bandits, each with a rifle slung from a strap behind one shoulder. Two have bandoliers loaded with bullets crisscrossing their chests. One wears the dark green mottled jacket of a mujahideen, and another the bright blue of the Taliban. It's difficult to know who they are, but I know they are dangerous.

Their conversation grows heated, and I wonder whether they are haggling over a price for the pears— or perhaps for the stolen truck—and hope their conversation will last long enough for me to get away. I press myself as flat as I can against the fruit to keep it from rolling under me. The pears are stacked higher near the front of the truck, so that the entire load is slanted upward from the opening in the canvas at the rear. Climbing uphill on my stomach over a shifting load of slippery, hard pears is no easy work.

The parting in the tarpaulin above the cab of the truck is too narrow to crawl through. The rain has tightened the knots in the ropes that hold the canvas flaps closed, and I cannot loosen them with my cold-stiff fingers. I find no hole that might tear if I pull at it hard enough. I fight to keep calm, telling myself that panic will make it harder to get away.

I find a dry rope inside the canvas tied to a ring over the driver's side of the cab, and I begin to work on it. My hands shake and my fingers move with painful slowness. One knot comes undone, but there are several more. A second comes loose. At that moment the voices are louder, and I peer back over my shoulder to see that one of the bandits has opened the canvas at the back of the truck to show the others the cargo.

I am in plain view at the top of the pile, and I

freeze with my head turned back over my shoulder, facing them. The rain clouds have parted and the sun has just risen over the bazaar. It shines brightly into their faces, and the inside of the truck is dim. They seem not to see me, and for the first time I feel lucky. I pray that they will close the canvas again quickly before their eyes adjust. But instead they argue over the price of the pears. I put my head down on my arm and lie perfectly still. Finally the canvas falls back into place and I no longer hear the men. I wipe a trickle of sweat from the side of my forehead and try to stop trembling.

The bandits have left the flap of the canvas untied. I wait for several minutes and then move toward the opening at the rear of the truck. When I am almost there, the men approach again and I don't dare look out for fear they will see me.

"Before we unload the fruit we will eat," one of them says, and other voices agree. I wait a few moments more and then very carefully look out to see the backs of the men disappearing into the crowd gathering in the bazaar.

Before slipping out of the truck, I stuff several of the pears into my shirt pockets, then pull the canvas aside. I have both feet out and am just pushing myself forward to jump to the ground when someone shouts, "Who's there?"

Below me and off to one side a boy about Nur's age—just a little older than me—rises to his feet. He does not have a beard, and his eyes look startled. He does not appear to have a gun. I jump to the ground and by the mercy of Allah land on my feet, which feel cramped and prickly after I've lain on hard pears all night. But I force them into motion and am lucky to dash in front of a wooden pony cart, startling the poor animal and making a temporary barrier between the boy and me.

"Stop!" he shouts. "Thief! Stop!" He runs after me, and I head down one of the covered lanes I spotted from the top of the truck. The boy is not far behind me, shouting "Thief! Stop!" again, and a few shopkeepers look up to see what the commotion is about. I run too fast for any of the surprised merchants to catch me, but they seem not to care about whether I've stolen something or whether I'm caught, which seems strange. After looking up for a moment out of curiosity, they bend back over their work.

The lane is filled with pyramids of vegetables. I dodge among early shoppers and men pushing handcarts until I find a break in the row of storefronts. I am about to duck into the empty space, where wooden crates and withered leaves of lettuce and cabbage are strewn over the ground. But it seems such an obvious place to hide that I am sure the boy will look for me there. Instead I keep on and enter a fruit stall a little farther down the lane, which is filling with women carrying string bags. I push my way through the crowd that mills about the shop so that I am hidden from the view of anyone passing in the lane. No one has seemed to notice me. My heart hammers inside my chest.

I wait for a long time because I have no way of knowing whether the boy has run past or is stopping to look inside each doorway. Finally I make my way to one side of the shop and manage to slip out through the curtain that hangs there. Once outside, I sit on an overturned crate to rest and wait for my heartbeat to return to normal.

It's difficult to believe I have made it safely to Peshawar! I have yet to learn where I might look for my father and brother, and I have no idea where I will find a safe place to sleep. Everything is uncertain and danger seems to be everywhere. But I am alive, which I had begun to believe would be impossible. For the first time in weeks I feel as if I have reason to be hopeful.

I spend most of the day wandering about the bazaar learning where things are. The fruit stalls are all together on one lane, flower vendors are on another alley next to the first, and on the other side is a lane of shops that sell vegetables. The bazaar is shaped like a wheel, with a hub at the center and the lanes radiating out like spokes. Footpaths thread between the lanes, and smaller footpaths with tiny cubbyholes of shops have grown from these. I begin to see the bazaar is as much like a spider web as a wheel. Across the hub are lanes where copper and brass smiths work. Near them are jewelry makers, row upon row of men blowing on little pipettes to direct the heat of small fires in metal dishes onto silver bars as they work exquisite scroll designs on earrings and pendants, goblets and plates.

Some lanes are lined with small factories with fires lit on open hearths, the smoke curling skyward. Lightbulbs hang from wires strung on poles suspended overhead. In several shops workers pump large, awkward bellows under glowing coals. They pull red-hot metal rods from the fire and hammer them into tools.

Beyond the tool bazaar are the cloth alleys, lane after lane of stores filled with everything from plain cottons to silks, and shops where beautiful wedding chadrs are embroidered with silver and gold and precious stones.

Many of the people in the bazaar are Afghans. Pashtu is the language I hear spoken the most, but Dari is almost as common. The familiarity of the words and the flow of the talk are comforting to me, as if I am not alone in the world after all. It gives me the courage to decide to ask someone where I might find shelter and where I might learn news of my father and brother.

I also think of asking the keepers of the larger shops whether I can earn money by sweeping or delivering things for them. But because I haven't spoken in such a long time, the first man I approach shakes his broom at me and chases me away before my mouth can form words. I am very hungry, and almost without thinking I grab a piece of fresh, hot onion bread from a basket on the counter before I run away. I fold the bread under my shirt and run down the alley and out of the bazaar. I walk until I find a large rock in an empty lot with a tree overhanging it, a place where I can sit out of sight to eat the bread.

A combination of hunger, fright, and shock that I have so easily resorted to stealing leaves me with shaking hands and knees. I tear at the bread with my teeth like an animal, and my throat feels raw when I swallow. I really have no choice, I tell myself. The shopkeeper had not been at all helpful and treated me like a thief just for trying to speak to him. I had to do it to keep from starving to death. Perhaps I will return after I've found work to pay the man for the bread I took. But then I think it might be better to stay away because if the owner sees me again he might beat me.

After I have eaten, I wander through a business district of taller buildings at the edge of the bazaar until I find the entrance to a lane where eggs and chickens are sold. I feel less exposed back inside the bazaar, and find a place under a handcart that is tipped up against the side of a building, where I sit and eat one of the pears. I watch the traffic pass, my eyes at the level of people's legs, and I am astonished at the range of footwear. There are soft leather boots, the kind that the Tajik merchants wear in Kunduz, cloth slippers embroidered with colored thread, and leather shoes that turn up at the toes, open-toed chappals, and high-heeled women's shoes with pointed toes, and rubber-soled canvas shoes. I never knew so many kinds of shoes existed, and I wonder who wears which kind. How do the women balance on the high heels?

Suddenly I feel very tired. Although it's only early afternoon, I'm exhausted from spending an entire night cold and uncomfortable on top of the truckload of pears. I have a desperate urge to sleep. I force myself to stay awake and think about where I will spend the night. The world here is very dangerous, filled with people who would as thoughtlessly and easily hurt me or murder me as if I were a dog. But my stomach is full, and it's not long before I doze off with my head on my arms, which curl around my knees.

I awake to shouting and cursing and a rough kick in the ribs. The owner of the cart has come to take it away. Without even thinking, I jump to my feet and turn to face the man. Again words will not come, but the shopkeeper isn't interested in any case, and raises his arm as if to strike me again. But I am quick and duck around him and easily get away.

I walk the rest of the day, looking for a place to sleep. It isn't until dark that the businesses in the fruit alley begin to close. Shops remain open in other lanes, but I watch and notice which fruit sellers sleep behind their counters, and which ones lock up their stalls with the produce inside before going away for the night. I see an elderly man with a shop that's no more than a cart without wheels and with shutters that fold down over the counter. The man sits in a small space behind the counter collecting money and putting fruit into small plastic bags to hand over to women in burqas. When he has sold all of his persimmons and oranges and apples, he pulls one shutter down, folds another one up, and fastens them together with a small brass padlock.

After the vendor has gone away, I walk around

to the back of his cart to examine it. It's at the end of a row, and the shops around it have already shut, so no one is nearby to notice me. The cart is very old, with spaces between the dried-out boards in its back wall. I duck behind it and with surprising ease am able to pry loose one of the boards and slip inside without anyone seeing me.

I lie awake for a time, listening to rats gnaw beneath me and worrying about whether I will awaken before the shopkeeper returns in the morning. But as tired as I am, nothing can keep me awake for more than a few minutes.

NUSRAT
Peshawar, Pakistan

15

*F*arid and Farooq are the first of Nusrat's students to go. One morning the bell outside the garden rings loudly, alarmingly, and before Husna can answer it the blue gate swings inward with a groan of its hinges. Standing on the other side is a tall, severe-looking man in a striped gray turban. As soon as they see him, Farid and Farooq jump to their feet and run to him, standing in front of him with eyes cast downward out of respect. They do it without joy—only with obedience, Nusrat thinks. She assumes this is the uncle from Kunduz who claimed that her teaching about the relationship of time and distance in space was "un-Islamic."

"I can't let them go with just anyone," says Nusrat to the intruder, purposefully neglecting to greet him.

"I am Mullah Tariq Gailani," says the stone-faced man, who also does not greet Nusrat or even his two nephews. "I am religious leader of the Northern Alliance forces in liberated areas of the North. I've come to take my brother's sons back to Kunduz with me."

Nusrat's heart skips a beat. "Have you any word from Mazar-i-Sharif?" she asks, her voice sounding more anxious than she'd meant it to. But she is desperate for news of Faiz and doesn't care what this mullah thinks. "Have you heard of an Afghan doctor at the clinic there? Dr. Faiz?"

"There is still much fighting in the North," the mullah says. "Many people have been killed by the American bombs falling from very high. But soon Mazar-i-Sharif also will be liberated." With that he turns, nudging the two boys in front of him like a mother hen, and walks through the gate.

Losing the boys sets Nusrat's teeth on edge. She had been attracted to Islam by its ancient affinity for order and knowledge. How ironic that this mullah is taking two of her best pupils away from their studies!

They're bright boys, and curious. They show great promise in their studies.

Nusrat goes to the gate and says goodbye. Farooq turns and smiles and offers her a formal salute. He does it shyly and Farid does the same. She feels as if her heart is falling to pieces. She remembers Farooq telling her about their village in Kunduz. "The houses are made of stones," he'd said. "Piled like this . . ." He made a pile of loose stones, which he nudged with his big toe, causing them to tumble. "Not good," he said. The North of Afghanistan is prone to earthquakes and many people die under the rubble of such houses. There is no school in their village, not even a madrassa, Farooq said.

They will return to their home, where they're shepherds, Nusrat thinks, a difficult life. Nusrat smiles at Farooq and Farid as she waves and calls after them, wishing them well, but her stomach aches as she watches their small square shoulders disappear down the alley beside her house. It pains her to think of the boys having too little to eat, no medical care, no education. So much potential wasted. For several days this is all she can think about. But the other students who stay claim her attention.

Mansoora takes to bringing Amina to school each day and staying through the morning. At first Nusrat thinks she comes for the food. But Mansoora loves the stories about the stars and seems to have an innate understanding of numbers. Mansoora has begun to speak, and to become more animated in every way.

One day Nusrat tells the class about the star Sirius, which produces over twenty times more light than the sun of our solar system and has inspired many cultures to name it the Dog Star. In these civilizations it was believed that when the sun's glare interfered with Earth's view of Sirius, natural calamities resulted. Mansoora stands to speak to the class.

"When I was a child in Helmand," she begins, "my father watched the Dog Star every night. It marched near the horizon in spring, and its constancy meant all was well in our world. But one summer night the Dog Star was not visible. The Helmand River flooded and wiped out our farm and the entire valley. It swept away our crops and the very dirt the crops grew in. What Madame Teacher, Muallem Saheba, says is true." Then with simple dignity Mansoora sits again.

That afternoon, when Mansoora and Amina leave, Nusrat takes Mansoora's hand and holds it for a moment.

"Thank you, Mansoora," she says, "for having faith in me. I'm so glad you have stayed to study."

"After the Taliban took my husband, I had no

hope," Mansoora replies. "I didn't know what would become of Amina and me until I came to the Persimmon Tree School. Now I know what will become of me. I will become a teacher like you." Nusrat smiles at her and squeezes her hand.

With six students still in Nusrat's class after the departure of Farooq and Farid, things go on as usual for about a week. But then one morning Tahira and Fariel don't appear. Nusrat dismisses her students early and goes to the Shahnawaz refugee camp to speak with Haroon about where the girls have gone and whether they'll be back. Inside the camp a guard takes her to wait behind a wall in the garden outside the malek's mud-brick house.

Sitting on a wood-and-string cot in the warm sunshine, Nusrat watches through the gate as people come and go in the camp. So many people walk on crutches. Many are missing a foot or a hand, victims of the anti-personnel and land mines, most of which date back to the Soviet war.

Nusrat is so infected by hope following the liberation of Kunduz, she's surprised at first to see how many people still move like automatons, staring straight ahead, their faces expressionless. She reminds herself that many of the refugees have been at Shahnawaz since the Soviet invasion in 1979, without jobs or money and with only what the government or the aid workers give them to eat. They no longer dream of returning home. Their children have been born here—a place without future, a dull limbo where time doesn't matter. These people have nothing to return to in Afghanistan.

A large crowd surrounds one mud-brick house, listening to the news on the radio. But the remarkable thing she notices is that the camp is filled with men—for once, there are more returned warriors with bandoliers across their chests and Kalashnikov rifles over their shoulders than elderly men and war invalids and boys too young to fight. The mujahideen stride back and forth, greeting each other loudly, clasping each other in great hugs of reunion and affection. They wear broad smiles, and small clutches of flowers stick out of the barrels of their guns.

Haroon comes out the front door of his house and touches his fingers to his forehead in a gesture of respect. They greet each other, and Haroon squats on his haunches beside the cot where Nusrat sits.

"Most of them have come from Kunduz," Haroon says, and they both watch the noisy crowds of men without speaking.

"I have come to ask about Tahira and Fariel, who didn't come to school today," says Nusrat, turning to the malek. "Their father is dead. Did someone take them back to Baghram?"

Haroon nods. "The girls' uncle came to take them back. The fighting has also stopped in Bamiyan and Baghram—so many places. It takes the mujahideen up to two weeks to walk here—and as you know, there are no roads into the areas where the fighting was. So it seems the Taliban are retreating. Some say they've come to Pakistan; some say they've taken up positions with foreign fighters in the caves of Tora Bora. There is still heavy fighting in Kandahar. The war is not over yet, although it seems to be over in the North. Even some of the mountain people from the North who have been here since the Soviets are going back."

Nusrat feels as if a cold hand squeezes her heart. If the war in the North is over, where is Faiz? If the fighters have come to take their families home, why hasn't he come? As she sits there, a man strolls past with his hand wrapped in the end of his turban. Blood drips to the ground. He smiles at his friend who walks beside him, as if he is not in danger of losing a hand. Haroon follows her gaze.

"So many injured by picking up the little yellow bombs," he says, referring to the unexploded canisters from the American cluster bombs. "They are the same color as the food packets, and a similar size." They watch the men as they disappear behind a row of tents.

Nusrat says goodbye to Haroon after extracting a promise that he will try to let her know which of her students will be going back to their homes inside Afghanistan. She makes her way through the refugee camp barely seeing the people who walk through the lanes in good humor, reunions happening outside of tent flaps, and people coming and going in every direction. The walk home is not far, but Nusrat wanders through the small bazaar just outside the development where her house sits.

If something terrible has happened to Faiz, surely they would have heard, she thinks, trying to calm herself. She makes her way to the queue of tongas at the end of her street and asks Basharat to take her to Asma and Sultan and Fatima, who she knows will restore her confidence.

NAJMAH
Peshawar, Pakistan

16

*T*he next morning I leave the bazaar, being careful to watch for landmarks that will show me how to get back. I follow behind some Afghan women and children who have come early to buy buffalo milk and are returning home. So many Afghans live in this city inside the border of Pakistan that I am certain I can find a community where people will tell me about those who were forced to fight with the Taliban and where I might look for my father and brother.

The women seem to glide over the ground, every part of them including their feet completely hidden under the flowing blue folds of burqas. They laugh and talk together and seem completely oblivious to their surroundings. I follow close behind them—close enough to hear the click of their heels on the pavement and the clink of their bangles under their robes. The children race ahead, chasing each other and coming back to beg their mothers for an apple or something else they want from the shops.

These sounds give me a strange sensation in the bottom of my stomach. In Baghlan and Faizabad and other cities, the Taliban whip women whose shoes make a sound on paving stones. And women hide their bangles away because if they're caught wearing jewelry it will be stolen and they will be beaten. My mother used to say women risk their lives by hiding their jewelry. They might even be stoned to death if it's found. Laughter also is forbidden, and these women laugh so that their voices sound like bells coming from inside their burqas.

Occasionally I catch a whiff of perfume wafting on the breeze that seems to follow close behind them. I think the rules must be very different in Peshawar. For I know the Taliban are here—I see them everywhere!

The women and children make several turnings in the lanes that radiate out from the bazaar, then, leaving the bazaar behind, they cross several busy streets and pass by a walled compound that contains hundreds of tents like the refugee settlement where I stayed with Akhtar and Khalida at Torkhum. I follow them to a tree-shaded, peaceful street lined with large bungalows that have stucco walls and gardens inside enclosed courtyards. They turn into a large, freshly painted house with a pair of elaborate wrought iron gates that clang shut behind them, and I continue down the street, as if I were a passerby. At the end of the street I go around the corner and head back toward the tent city of refugees.

Only one pair of gates leads into and out of the tent city. I walk past several times, watching as dozens of people enter and leave through those gates, some in pairs, some singly, others in clumps of four or five. I build my confidence to speak to the guard. Although I am sure that I can speak, the thought of it overwhelms me. My silence has protected me, saved my life, and I am afraid to let go of it.

Finally I walk up to the gate and stand right in front of the guard posted there. He is dressed in a tattered Punjabi dereshi, a tan woolen vest, and a rolled-up woolen pakul hat. He ignores me at first, but I stand squarely in front of him, and finally he looks me in the face. I open my mouth to speak, but nothing will come out.

"What do you want?" he snarls at me in Pashtu.

My eyes shift past him into the walled area of tents. The guard lifts his arm and points in the direction of the largest mud-walled house in the compound, a house very similar to the one where the malek lived in Torkhum.

I slip through the gate quickly without asking, not wanting to give the guard an opportunity to turn me away. Inside the compound the dust lies as thick in the air as it does on the backs of the donkeys. The smell of garbage and sewage is strong. Children run through the spaces among the tents and women squat beside their open tent flaps visiting with their neighbors, just as they'd done at Torkhum. I go right up to the malek's wooden door before I can stop to think of how I should behave and make him understand me without speaking, for I am less sure now whether I will be able to say a word. I rap quickly on the door. A gray-bearded man with amber eyes opens the door and steps outside.

He greets me and I blink. My throat aches with wanting to tell him what has happened to my mother and Habib and how desperate I am to find my father and Nur. But I cannot make a sound.

"Where did you come from?" the malek asks. He looks at me carefully, his eyes shifting from the top of my head down to my feet, and back again. Suddenly I remember I am covered in dust. I have not bathed since two days or more before I left Torkhum, I don't know how many days in all. I brush at my sleeves, but it sends up a cloud so thick it makes me sneeze. In the pouch tied at my waist I carry the folded sheet of paper that Akhtar wrote out with my name on it. But I cannot bring myself to give it to the malek.

I shake my head, and my shoulders begin to swivel of their own accord. Before I can stop myself, I am turning my shoulders and shaking them in the same rhythm as my head.

"Where is your family?" he asks. My body continues to swivel and sway. I cannot answer him, no matter how hard I try.

"Where are you staying?" Again I cannot answer. But this time I am glad because I am certain that staying in the bazaar is not allowed. I take a deep breath.

"Can you work?" he asks. Suddenly I know how to answer, and my body stops swiveling and swaying. I nod my head vigorously and hold out my hands so he can see the calluses on my palms and fingers from carrying firewood and water and cutting grass. He runs his finger over them and smiles.

"So! You can earn your keep," he says softly. I try to will him to say that I can stay with him and his family. I need a place to feel safe and someone who will be kind to me and help me to find what remains of my family. And then I'm afraid again because I know if I were to stay with him or any other proper family in a house, the first thing that would happen is that I would be made to bathe. And then it would be known that I am a girl. After the dangers of the last days, I want to feel secure, but I must keep my identity as a boy.

"First," says the malek, "we should find you a place to stay. Do you go to school?" I shake my head. I wanted to study, but the Taliban shut down the schools in our village and all the villages of Kunduz. There were no schools for girls, and the only school for boys was the madrassa, where the mullahs were very strict and taught people to hate. My father would not allow Nur to go to the madrassa.

"No matter," says the malek. "Many of the students in this school have never been to classes before. The teacher is an American, and she feeds the students every day. Perhaps you could do work for her and she would let you sleep there. I don't know what she can do with a child who doesn't speak."

Again I show him the palms of my hands and point to the thick ridge of calluses at the base of my fingers, formed by hauling water up the hill from the Baba Darya. This makes the malek laugh, and he pats my shoulder.

He tells me to wait outside his house while he makes the rounds of the tent city to solve some problems and check on new arrivals and the distribution of food and water. He gives me some water and tells me to sit on a cot under a tree in the courtyard at the back of his house. No one else seems to be in the house, and I wonder about the malek's family. Perhaps they were killed in the bombing, as my mother and Habib were. I am sorry for him. But if he has a wife she might make me change my clothes, and then I would no longer be safe.

When the malek returns, he beckons to me and I follow behind him as he walks through the camp. I try to make note of the small distinctions in the turnings among the tents, many of which are an identical greenish-brown canvas. I count five rows and then a turn to the right.

The last rows of tents are the oldest. From a distance they look as if they have skin peeling from them the way skin peels when it's been too long exposed to the sun. When I get closer, I see they are covered with tattered plastic bags from the bazaar, stitched to the tents to keep the rain out. Around these tents the people stand like many others I've seen, looking at you with eyes that have nothing behind them. Many are missing a hand or a foot or an eye. So many of them have terrible wounds and scars. Some have open sores. You can tell by looking at them that they have little food and no clean water, and the only thing they live on is dreams of their farms, which no longer exist.

We walk past row after row of tents, and in older parts of the camp the tents have been replaced by mud-brick houses. Everywhere the people stare into space without noticing who passes, and then we are outside the refugee camp and in the city again. We walk in the same direction I'd taken earlier following the women to the house with the ornate metal gate. We pass the street where I turned behind the women and continue on to an area where the houses are smaller and less well kept.

NUSRAT
Peshawar, Pakistan

17

*I*t is a cool, sunny day and the class works at division problems on their wooden chalkboards while Nusrat helps Husna bring out the noonday meal. The table is in place, and Husna carries trays of food. Nusrat is moving aside the chalkboard and easel, when the bell at the gate jangles. It so often rings at mealtime, Nusrat thinks.

She is not surprised to see Haroon outside the garden wall, and standing beside him a tall slender boy with watchful eyes. Most often when the bell rings at mealtime, it's Haroon bringing a new student. The boy's shoulders swivel nervously, and Nusrat regards him carefully before opening the gate. He is perhaps ten or eleven years old. His eyes are outlined in heavy black surmeh—and his mouth is wide, showing even, white teeth clamped firmly on the embroidered tail end of a broad silk turban to keep it from sailing away on the wind. Head to foot, clothing and skin, he is the color of dust.

"Ah-salaam-aleikum," says Nusrat, pushing the gate open. Haroon greets her and she asks, "Are you hungry?" As usual, Haroon shakes his head. But the boy's eyes remain fixed on the table of food as if he hasn't eaten once in all of his short life.

"This boy does not speak," says Haroon. "No doubt he has seen terrible things. I think he has just arrived from somewhere in the North of Afghanistan. At least, I haven't seen him before." The boy's eyes flicker to Haroon's face for a second, then fly back to the table of food. "And he seems to be alone. Do you have room for him?"

"Yes," says Nusrat, "of course. Come in." She gestures toward the rough wooden table where the other children have stopped their gnawing to turn and stare at the new arrival.

Haroon touches his forehead with his fingertips and backs out of the gate, saying "Khuda-hafez"— God look after you—and bowing slightly. Nusrat says goodbye to him hastily. Her attention is focused on the boy, whose eyes move from plate to plate, lingering on the kebabs. "Come in," says Nusrat. "Sit down and eat. If you've come to study, you can't do it on an empty stomach."

He glides through the garden as if he's drawn on a stream of air, and Nusrat thinks, "This child also is a shepherd." His feet seem barely to touch the ground, and his eyes never leave the plates of food. Nusrat leads him to the table.

The others watch as he eats hungrily, without bothering to sit. He watches them back over a second kebab. Husna fetches him a tumbler of water from the pitcher she's refilled at the earthenware filter urn on a table in the corner of the garden near the washstand. He lowers his eyes only when she hands him the water. When he is finished, Nusrat hands him the damp pink towel to wipe his hands and mouth.

"What's your name?" Nusrat asks the boy. "Would you like more?" He shakes his head and suddenly seems shy. He doesn't answer.

"You don't talk or you can't talk?" she asks him gently, and color rises under the dust on his cheeks. He shakes his head only once, but the movement is emphatic. Nusrat pats him on the shoulder. "It doesn't matter," she says. "You can listen, and that's all that counts here."

Unlike the clothes of most of the children in the

camp, the boy's are new under their thick coating of dust. His tunic and trousers are too large. They are rolled up at the cuffs and sleeves, and his toes are hidden inside his sandals. Most refugee children wear clothing that has been handed down several times. They wear everything until it is more holes than fabric, or until it doesn't cover their growing bodies any longer, and then is passed on to the next smaller child. New clothes are unusual.

"Are you here to learn numbers?" Nusrat asks. He blinks and doesn't answer. "Would you like to sit down?" She gestures to the wooden cots, where the others sit. He watches Nusrat intently, walking backward slowly until the edge of the cot hits the backs of his legs, forcing him to sit suddenly in a space vacated when Ahmed and Wali scoot apart to make room.

The wind gusts. Dust flies into their faces, leaving their teeth gritty. The air has grown colder, and the sky is suddenly an angry blue-gray. While Husna clears the lunch and drags the table away, Nusrat carries the old easel with the chalkboard on it to the open space at the head of the U and taps it with her pointer to get the attention of her students.

Just then a gust of dust-laden wind blows the chalkboard over, and this time when Nusrat rights it, the wind topples it again. The children take advantage of the disturbance and begin laughing and shoving at each other. The new boy draws himself in, as if to keep from touching the boy on either side of him. To add to the confusion, large drops of rain splat into the dust of the garden and the children help Nusrat drag the cots under the shelter of the stoop outside the kitchen door before running for their makeshift homes in the refugee camps.

"Remember division," Nusrat calls after them. "I'll ask you about division first thing tomorrow. Chicken for dinner—and I will tell you another star story!" She turns to hurry inside as the wind pushes the rain so hard it flies sideways and stings her face. She nearly collides with the strange new boy, who stands under the shelter of the kitchen stoop, his hands clasped as if to keep them from fluttering away.

"Aren't you going home?" Nusrat asks him. He shakes his head so hard his turban wobbles. "Where are your family?" she asks, and he shakes his head again, this time swiveling his shoulders along with his head, not stopping until she leans down so that her face is level with his, and she can see that tears make runnels in the dust caked at the sides of his eyes.

Nusrat clasps him firmly against her, her arm circling his thin shoulders, and guides him inside the bungalow, through the kitchen. Husna turns to watch as Nusrat leads him, her arm still around his shoulders, into the hallway, and through it to the sitting room at the front of the bungalow. A horse pulls a wooden cart loaded with firewood past the gate in the thick stucco wall that hems in the strip of yard outside the front window. Hooves and wooden wheels squelch in the already muddy street.

Nusrat points to a chair with horsehair stuffing and cotton batting visible through the worn damask on its seat. The boy looks at the chair dubiously and sits cautiously, facing the window. Nusrat pulls up a smaller wooden chair to sit in front of him so she can look into his face in the silvery light from the window.

"So," she says, wiping the tears from his cheeks with the flat of her hand, a gesture that seems so motherly that her throat closes. "Do you need a place to stay?" The boy nods his head slowly.

Nusrat reaches into a bowl on the table that stands in front of the window beside their chairs and picks up a bright orange persimmon that sits on top of a pyramid of ripe fruit. She takes the boy's hand and turns it palm up to place the fruit in it. She runs her finger over the calluses at the base of his fingers and below the center knuckles and looks up into his eyes, which watch her intently as she places the fruit in the cup of his palm and curls his fingers up over it.

"Well," says Nusrat. "Don't worry. I wish you could tell me about yourself—where you've come from and how you got here. It will help us to locate your family." The boy begins to turn the fruit over and over in his fingers.

He looks at her with troubled eyes, the surmeh smeared in black smudges that blend with dirt. Solemnly he reaches into a pouch tied around his waist under his tunic and pulls something out of it. He drops it onto the tabletop beside the bowl of fruit and resumes turning the fruit in his fingers. At first Nusrat thinks it's a small, light pebble, but she picks it up and holds it in the light, and sees the webs and crinkles of a small wad of paper.

"What's this?" she asks, and his eyes stay locked on hers while she attempts to unfold the paper without tearing it. When she has opened it and smoothed it flat against the table, she reaches under the fringed shade of the lamp to turn on the light. She can barely read the smudged and faded pencil marks for the creases. She turns it this way and that.

"S-H-A-H-E-E-D," she reads finally, and the boy's eyes are still clamped on her face.

"Whose name is this?" she asks, and his eyes dart about the room. "Shaheed means 'martyr,'" she says, and he nods once, definitely. "Why is it not Shaheeda?" Shaheeda is the female form of the name.

The child stands and looks quickly around the room as if searching for an escape route. Nusrat reaches out and takes this girl-dressed-as-a-boy gently by the wrists and holds her that way until she sits again. The teacher leans forward to speak so that their eyes meet.

"You're safe here," she says. "But it is very dangerous for you to pretend you're a boy. You must stop or you will become a martyr! Now tell me your real name."

The girl continues to stare at her, and she tries to pull her hand free from Nusrat's grasp. "You mustn't be frightened," says Nusrat. "Please be still and let us see if I can help you. You will be safe here, and you can stay as long as you need to stay." Najmah stops struggling but continues to watch with eyes that brim with suspicion.

"How did you know?" says Najmah, her voice a hoarse whisper.

"So you *can* talk! I'm so relieved. It will be much easier to help you if I know more about you. I knew you were a girl because of the way your hands are callused. Your work is carrying wood and cutting grass and sweeping, is it not?" she asks. Najmah nods once. "That is girls' work," says Nusrat. She opens her own hand and shows Najmah her own calluses in identical places on her fingers.

"Now," says Nusrat, "what is your real name?" She reaches out and gently removes the turban to reveal hair that is brutally shorn in chunks and patches. Najmah's hands fly to her head as if she tries to protect it from blows. Nusrat waits patiently for her to speak, and Najmah runs her hands from her forehead over the crown and down the back of her head, one hand after the other, over and over again.

"Najmah," she whispers. "My name is Najmah."

Nusrat sits quietly for a few moments, giving Najmah time to calm herself. Then she leans forward and takes one of Najmah's hands between her own.

"Star," Nusrat says softly; "such a beautiful name." Najmah nods her head several times and pulls away her hand. When she speaks, her voice is rough and quiet.

"My father gave me my name," says Najmah. "He loves the stars, and he taught me and my brother, Nur, to love them, too."

"And tell me where your father and Nur are," says Nusrat.

Najmah's face crumples like the paper that sits so delicate and insubstantial on the table beside them.

NUSRAT / NAJMAH
Peshawar, Pakistan

18

The storm cuts out the electricity, and so Nusrat lights an oil lamp in the kitchen and takes Najmah back to the bedroom across the hall from her own room when it's still early. The light from the window has faded to dimness through the reed blinds, and the girl looks sleepy.

"Here is where you will sleep," says Nusrat. "Stay awake just a little longer and we'll get you a bath and some fresh clothes and a meal, and then you can sleep."

Nusrat calls Husna and counts out some rupees to take to the bazaar to buy Najmah a skirt and a kameez. "Take Basharat and his son with you," she says. Even with the Taliban defeated in parts of Afghanistan, it's not safe for a woman to walk alone in the bazaar in Peshawar. Still, a woman and man walking together might be accosted and asked for proof that they're married. If there is no proof, they could be beaten, or worse. A child will divert suspicion from Husna and Basharat.

"Najmah can wear one of my sweaters, and I have many scarves," she says. "We can find one that's a good color to go with whatever you buy."

They return to the kitchen, and Nusrat invites Najmah to sit at the table while she fills a bucket at the pump in the sink. She starts a fire on the iron stove and heats the water for Najmah's bath. Najmah wants to help, but she is so tired she can barely keep her eyes open. She sits at the table with her roughly shorn head resting on one arm and her eyes fluttering to stay open.

"Your hair was cut in a hurry?" Nusrat asks. It sticks up in unruly tufts, and some longer locks are interspersed with much shorter ones. Najmah blinks and sits up straight. She nods her head. Nusrat puts down the bucket and comes to the table to sit facing Najmah.

"Really, you are safe here," Nusrat says. "I don't want to make you talk if you don't want to. But I need to know what happened to your family so I can help you find them. Do you understand?" Najmah blinks again and studies Nusrat's face carefully before nodding slowly. Nusrat smiles and reaches for Najmah's hands, but the girl pulls back. Nusrat stands and picks up the bucket filled with cold water.

Najmah follows her back and forth between the kitchen and the bathroom as Nusrat fills the plastic tub in the bathroom with two buckets of cold water, then brings the pot of boiling water in to add to it to make the bathwater warm. Nusrat leaves a large clean folded towel, a soft, belted robe, and a piece of soap in a dish on a small square table beside the wooden pallet. She explains to Najmah that she will stand on the pallet and ladle the warm water over herself, use the soap, and rinse herself over the drain. Then, when she's clean, she can climb into the plastic tub and sit in the warm water.

"You will sleep much better afterward," Nusrat says.

On the wide stone windowsill of the bathroom is another oil lamp. Najmah is used to bathing in cold water from a cup while standing on a little bed of stones in the dark behind her family's house in Kunduz. The drain and pallet and the tubful of warm water look complicated and unimaginably extravagant to her.

When Nusrat has finished pouring water and laying out the things for Najmah's bath, she leaves her guest to undress and bathe.

"I'll have some warm food for you in the kitchen when you're ready," she says as she leaves the room, pausing as she pulls the door closed behind her. She turns toward Najmah. "I'm very happy you're here with me," she says. "We will talk about your family when you're ready. And I will help you look for them if that's what you want."

/

At first I'm too tired to be able to speak. My voice seems to come only with great effort. Also, the teacher's words jolt me—it's hard to imagine that a small, weak yellow-haired foreigner would be able to help find Baba-jan and Nur. Her kindness is difficult to accept after learning not to trust anyone these last weeks. I nod slowly at her, but I am afraid to talk to her about Baba-jan and Nur. I may be safe with her for the moment, but I don't know if I'll ever feel comfortable.

I feel very much as I felt when I climbed into the truck filled with pears at Torkhum. I'm not sure what will happen next, but I have no one else to trust and no other choices. I cannot sleep in the bazaar—it's too dangerous. I will have to decide later whether this woman really can help me, and whether she can protect me. For now I will say nothing and I will take things as they come.

I wash and rinse myself as the teacher showed me. When I climb into the tub, and the warm water makes my skin tingle with pleasure, sleep seems like the only thing I could ever want. A knock on the door makes my scalp prickle and I am just as alert again as if I'd never been tired.

"You can just leave your clothes in the tashnab, and Husna will wash them tomorrow," says the teacher through the wooden door. She speaks Dari— not the sweet-sounding Persian of my mountain people but the Persian of the plains, which I understand, although it is harsh to my ears. If I could not see the foreign teacher, I would judge by her voice and language that she was Afghan—perhaps from Kabul. But I would know she was not one of us.

The warm water relaxes me, and once again I can think only of sleep. I step out of the tub, and the cool air awakens me again. When I have dried myself, I wrap the strange large garment the teacher has left around myself and tie it in the middle. I take the oil lamp and go out into the hallway, holding it high so that I can see into the sleeping rooms that face each other across the hallway at the end of the bungalow.

Both of these rooms have very large cots in them, each of which could hold my entire family.

The house is many times larger than our house in Kunduz. Our house would have fit into any one of these rooms. But compared to the other houses the malek and I passed on the street, this one is small, with only the two sleeping rooms, a tashnab, a salon, and a kitchen. My family slept all together in the main room of our house. It must feel very strange to sleep in a room all alone, and stranger still in such a large cot—strange and lonely. I think of the chickens and the bukri that were always underfoot in our house, their soft sounds part of the song of our lives.

I tiptoe past the salon and peer around the corner and into the kitchen at the back of the house, where the yellow-haired foreigner stands at the strange metal stove stirring something pungent. The servant comes in through the back door carrying some parcels. She sets them down and sweeps her burqa from her head, dropping it onto a chair beside the wooden table in the center of the kitchen.

"It's very cold," says the servant, whose voice is sour and bitter. Then she sees me standing in the hallway with the oil lamp. When the teacher sees the servant looking at me, she turns and puts down the large wooden spoon she's been stirring with and smiles.

She pulls out a chair and motions me to sit. Chairs are very strange to me. I don't like sitting so far off the floor.

"Come," says the teacher. "Sit. I will have your food on the table in a minute. When you've finished, you can go to sleep if you'd like. Husna has brought you some clothes for the morning."

I sit on the chair beside the bare-topped table, and the teacher sits across from me. The servant woman takes over at the stove, and I can tell she listens to every word we speak. The kitchen is warm, but drafts of chilly air sweep through. I pull the strange garment around myself more tightly and wish for my pattu.

"So," says the teacher, "Husna and I are very happy to have you stay here with us for as long as you'd like." I think she says this for the benefit of the servant, since she has already told me. Husna turns her head over her shoulder and casts a wary eye on me.

"Would you like that?" the yellow-haired one asks. I blink my eyes and then nod my head. Once again I find it difficult to speak. Again I hold my hands out to show her my calluses. She rubs her fingertips over them, at the base of each finger and below the middle knuckles. Then she folds my hands together and holds them between her large, very white hands.

"I know that you can work very hard," she says. "But the work I want you to concentrate on is school-work. We will have some things for you to do—you can help carry water and perhaps run some errands. But I want you to study. Do you understand?" Again I blink my eyes. I'm not sure that I do understand.

"We will give you a place to sleep and all that you need to eat. But I'd like you to study your numbers and learn to read and write. Does that suit you?" I nod my head. It suits me very well, but I can barely believe my ears. She's giving me a safe, clean place to sleep, food, and an opportunity to go to school. Surely she will ask something in return!

The servant puts plates on the table and serves chicken and naan and pillau and steaming spiced vegetables. There is enough food for a wedding feast—far more than the three of us could ever eat.

The teacher sits while I eat vegetables and pillau. I ignore the knife and fork beside my plate, eating with my right hand, mashing peas and potatoes together, and sopping up gravy with pieces of naan. I slurp sweet green tea in over my teeth, and the teacher smiles. I think she approves of my good manners.

When I finish eating, she gives me a glass of cold milk. I am able to drink only half.

"You may call me Nusrat," the teacher says. "And you may call Husna by her name as well." I nod to show that I understand. "I will prepare your bed for you so that you can sleep." She pats my hand again and leaves the room.

Husna bustles about, clearing the table, her mouth set in a rigid line.

"You should call her Khanum Faiz, Mrs. Faiz," she mutters, "or Muallem Saheba, madame teacher." She bangs the bowl in her hands down on the table, and the noise makes me jump. "She's a married lady and a respected teacher. You should not take advantage of her kindness."

I say nothing, but I stare at this bitter woman and wonder why she should be so angry with me. I decide I will call the teacher Bibi Nusrat, a term of respect and affection. I like her name. I will not speak to the servant at all.

NAJMAH / NUSRAT
Peshawar, Pakistan

19

The next morning I awaken to the sound of a rooster crowing in the garden, and for a moment I imagine I'm at home in Kunduz. The dream stays with me until I raise my hand and feel the stubble of my hair and realize with a start that I am in a strange bed in Pakistan with a strange, kind woman in control of my fate.

I push back the covers and am startled to see that Bibi Nusrat is sitting on a chair beside the bed watching me. Next to her on a small wooden table is a pot of tea under an embroidered woolen cozy and a plate of strange white biscuits that look as if they are filled with fat sulaiman.

"Chai?" she asks, and I nod. I try to get out of bed, but the quilt tangles around my legs and feet. There is a thin sheet under the quilt—or quilts—and the bed is much softer than a quilt on the ground, which is what I'm used to. I feel rested and groggy. Nusrat holds out a cup of steaming green tea. It's scented with cardamom, the way my mother prepares it for special occasions, such as when we have important guests. The largest and best cardamom comes from India, and is expensive. It's difficult to get, impossible in wartime.

"You will come to class today?" asks Bibi Nusrat, moving to sit beside me on the edge of the cot. It sounds like a question, but I'm quite sure it is not. "I'll try to make your hair look better," she says, running her hand over my head. I duck away from her hand, but she ignores it. "Your clothes are in the cupboard." She nods over her shoulder at a door in the wall at the end of the room. I try to smile at her. She is very kind, but I still do not want to be touched and I do not yet want to talk about my family.

/

Nusrat lays out the tunic and skirt and a blue scarf before collecting the cups and tea tray and leav-

[*206*]

ing Najmah to dress. After breakfast Husna prepares the midday meal, and Nusrat is dragging the cots under the persimmon tree when Najmah emerges from her room with the scarf draped around her head. Nusrat hands her a wooden chair to take out into the courtyard and follows her with a comb and pair of scissors to even out the tufts and knobs of hair on Najmah's head.

When Nusrat has finished, she shakes out the towel she's draped around Najmah's shoulders and hands the girl a mirror. In America this would be a chic, boyish cut, Nusrat thinks. But here such a haircut is scandalous. Najmah looks at her image, puts down the mirror, and rubs her hands repeatedly over her head from her brow, over the crown, and down the back. Nusrat takes her hands and stills her.

"It will grow quickly," she says with an understanding smile. Najmah pulls her hands away and folds them in her lap.

"The Taliban forced my father and brother to fight with them," Najmah says in a husky voice. She stares at her hands, and Nusrat sits on the wooden cot facing Najmah. "I worried that Baba-jan's beard was not long enough, and they would think he was not a good Muslim. They accused us of helping their enemies, and they took all of our food." She continues to stare into her lap. "I don't know whether

Baba-jan and my brother, Nur, are still alive, or where they are. I came alone from Kunduz."

Nusrat does not try to touch the girl. Najmah's words take Nusrat's breath away. It's hard to imagine the terrible things she has seen. It is too difficult to visualize a girl of this age making her way to Pakistan alone on foot, dressed as a boy. Najmah tells her a little about the journey without looking at the teacher once, and Nusrat sits silently listening to her.

"The last thing my father said to my mother as he was taken away was that she should stay, no matter what happens," Najmah says. "He was afraid they'd take our house, our land, and our sheep."

"And did she? Stay?" Nusrat asks. Najmah nods and looks around the garden before speaking, as if to be certain no one else is there. Husna comes outside carrying the washstand and table with water tumblers, and Najmah waits for her to go back into the kitchen before speaking again.

"She was running, carrying my baby brother to the house. I ran toward them down the hill. I couldn't hear the airplanes, which were very high above us, but the earth was jumping all around our house. I shouted to my mother. Then suddenly I was on the ground, covered with dirt and rocks." She tells Nusrat the entire story in a flat tone with no feelings showing through the simple, horrible words.

Nusrat sits very still while Najmah tells her about putting on Akhtar's clothes, walking with him and his family to the border crossing, and getting into the truck filled with pears, which had brought her to Peshawar.

"Where did you sleep before you came here?" asks Nusrat. A deep pink spreads across Najmah's cheeks and creeps down her neck. She tells Nusrat about the cart owner and his threat to beat her if he sees her again, and about sleeping in the fruit stall.

"Does Haroon know about your father and brother?" Nusrat asks. Najmah shakes her head.

"It's difficult to know who to trust. I don't know that I can trust you. But I have no choice. If nobody knows my story, then my father and brother will not find me—if they're still alive. So I had to let my tongue tell you this story."

"You can trust me," says Nusrat quietly. "Many fighters are going to the Shahnawaz camp to look for their relatives because the Taliban have left Kunduz." Najmah watches her carefully but says nothing. "Perhaps your father and brother will look for you there. We should tell Haroon. He will let us know if he hears news of your father and brother." Najmah folds her arms and hugs herself but does not speak.

"The malek is a good man, Najmah," says Nusrat. "He will help you if he can, but first he must know your story. Other people from your village must be in the refugee camps and they may have news." Najmah swallows, and her eyes dart about the room.

"I won't speak to Haroon unless you want me to," Nusrat says quickly, and Najmah relaxes her shoulders. "I know how difficult it is to trust anyone after what's happened to you. But you must let me help—I shudder to think how dangerous it was for you to pretend to be a boy and make your way here alone. You look nothing like a boy—it's a wonder anyone believed you at all."

"I had no choice," says Najmah.

"Of course you didn't," says Nusrat. "Life is difficult enough for a girl, impossible for a girl on her own."

"I fooled enough people to get me here," says Najmah, "and I will fool enough to get me back. Whether you find my father and brother or not, I must return to my village as my father desired." Her face takes on a sharp line at the jaw.

It's Nusrat's turn to be quiet. She stands and rearranges the cots she has set up for the students under the persimmon tree. She arranges bolsters and cushions on them, and then she sits again across from the straight-backed chair where Najmah sits.

"Do you have other family members who may

have come from Kunduz?" the teacher asks. Najmah shakes her head.

"I have an uncle," she says. "But my heart does not recognize him as a member of my family. When the Taliban took the other men away, they allowed Uncle to stay in the village, and I do not trust him." Nusrat looks at her closely.

"Is your uncle your enemy?" she asks, and Najmah nods. "If your father and brother are dead, what will be in the village for you?" asks Nusrat. "Especially if you have an enemy there. You weren't safe when your mother was alive—what chance will you have alone?" Najmah's gaze does not waver and she shakes her head. Nusrat leans back in her chair. Najmah appraises the teacher's blond hair and fair skin.

"You are not Muslim," Najmah says. "I do not expect you to understand."

"But I am Muslim," Nusrat says. "I married a doctor from Afghanistan. He came back here out of love for his family and his country, and I came with him. I understand very well." Nusrat is quiet for a moment.

"What is the name of your village?" she asks.

"Golestan," Najmah answers.

"In any case, the first thing is to find out what has become of your father and your brother," Nusrat says. Najmah nods, and Husna comes out of the kitchen just as the bell rings at the gate.

Ahmed and Wali arrive first and sit on the cot. Before long they are laughing and tumbling like two puppies. After Mansoora and Amina arrive and the boys have quieted, Nusrat asks them to review the lesson on division from the day before. She half listens while she looks over their heads to the open kitchen door to see whether Najmah will join them.

Beside the kitchen door Husna keeps a large curry bush growing in a clay pot. Behind the shadowed movement of air through oval leaves Nusrat sees the outline of her in her kameez and scarf, listening out of sight.

Their lesson has been under way for only a few minutes when there is a disturbance at the gate. Nusrat crosses the garden and peers over the wall. Haroon stands beside the gate arguing with a broad-chested, bearded stranger in an extravagantly wound black turban.

"Ho!" Haroon calls out when he sees Nusrat. The teacher motions to Amina to continue speaking, and opens the gate a crack to greet the two men. She stands in the way of their view into the garden without inviting them inside. Nusrat has grown wary of strangers wearing black turbans, since many of the religious zealots wear them.

"This is Engineer Mohiuddin Baghlani," says Haroon. "He is looking for his niece, an orphan from Kunduz." Nusrat feels as if a large piece of dry bread is stuck in her throat, and she swallows instead of answering. "He thought perhaps, since children come here to your garden, the girl might have come . . ." Haroon goes on. Nusrat turns and looks over her shoulder at the children under the persimmon tree and stands aside so the men can peer into the garden.

"Do you see her here?" she asks the man. A spot twitches between her shoulder blades, and she prays that Najmah will stay hidden in the kitchen.

Beneath the broad-shouldered stranger's large turban sit a pair of humorless eyes that come to rest on Amina and Mansoora. He grunts and turns toward Haroon, who studies the dirt in front of his sandals.

"If you should see a tall, dark-haired girl of about twelve, please let me know," says Haroon.

"What village in Kunduz?" Nusrat asks, not addressing the man directly. "In case such a child comes, I can ask," she adds quickly. There must be many uncles looking for their brothers' children, Nusrat thinks. Still, her heart races and she glances toward the kitchen, where the outline of the sleeve and scarf are no longer visible behind the curry bush.

"Golestan," says the stranger, narrowing his eyes.

"What does this man want with his niece?" Nusrat asks of Haroon. She doesn't want to address the stranger directly because she doesn't want to antagonize him and she does not want to sound as if she might not approve of his intentions. Haroon speaks in a low voice to the stranger and turns back to Nusrat.

"He wants to take her back to live in her village with his family," Haroon tells her. "He will claim his dead brother's property. She will live in the house where she grew up, in sh'Allah."

"God willing," Nusrat repeats softly. "If I see the girl, I will tell you, Haroon." She nods toward the stranger and turns back to her students.

"Memsaheb," says Haroon politely, "where is the boy I brought to you yesterday?" Without missing a heartbeat, Nusrat smiles pleasantly.

"He found his family, Khuda-ra-shukur," she says.

"Yes," says Haroon, "Khuda-ra-shukur, thank God."

Nusrat turns to her students, who have abandoned their discussion of long division. The children are running about the garden, laughing and shouting. There is no sign of Najmah, and she thinks the girl must have heard her uncle's voice, and she wonders whether she heard him say her father is dead.

Najmah's disappearance from the kitchen also tells Nusrat that she wants nothing to do with her uncle—even if he would take her back to her village—and Nusrat decides she must protect her in any way necessary.

In the children's jostling the easel and chalkboard have fallen to the ground, and also the tray with the metal water tumblers. The boys help her pick things up, and when they're seated again Nusrat looks up to see Najmah sitting on the cot beside Amina and Mansoora, facing the cot that holds the boys. Ahmed and Wali stare at her uncertainly, quiet for once.

"This is Najmah," says Nusrat, walking behind the girl to place a hand on her shoulder. Najmah stares at her feet encased in the too-large sandals that Akhtar gave her the day her mother and Habib had died. "You saw her yesterday dressed as a boy."

"Why was she—" Wali begins to ask, but Ahmed pokes him with an elbow to silence him.

To distract them, Nusrat tells them to wash their hands for dinner. She sends Najmah to help Husna carry out trays, which contain salt-roasted chicken and naan.

After they have eaten, Amina and Wali and

Ahmed play in the garden, running and swinging on the blue-painted gate. Mansoora and Najmah help clear the table away. When Nusrat calls her students back to the cots under the persimmon tree, Najmah takes her place again. She shows no sign that she thinks her father and brother are dead.

As soon as the other students leave, Nusrat takes Najmah into the kitchen and asks her to sit at the kitchen table. She sits across from her. "Did you hear what your uncle said?" Nusrat asks. Najmah nods and folds her hands in front of her.

"I believe that my father and brother are alive," she says after a while. "If they've been killed, how would Uncle know it? I don't believe anything he says."

"Why won't you go back to Kunduz with your uncle?" asks Nusrat.

"He will take me back and force me to marry someone. He will send me away and he will take my father's land. My father did not want him to have our farm any more than he wanted the Taliban to have it." Najmah speaks bitterly.

Nusrat thinks of Najmah married and having babies before her body is grown, dying old at a tender age in a mountain village. Most people in Afghanistan do not live to be forty-five years old. She marvels at the courage of this strange girl named Star.

"We can't ask Haroon's help with finding your father and brother now," Nusrat says. "I'm certain he'll think that sending you off with your uncle would be the best thing to do." Najmah stares at her interlaced fingers and doesn't respond. "You can't go back to Kunduz alone, the way you got here. It's too dangerous. It's only a matter of time until Haroon learns you're here." Najmah does not answer.

Nusrat is weary when she lies down on her bed that night, but she knows she will not sleep. She replays the scenes of Najmah's story and thinks how terrible life has been for the people of Afghanistan for the last twenty-five years. Somehow looking at this bright young girl and hearing her story in her own words makes the terribleness more real and immediate than it has seemed before.

She thinks of the horrors Faiz has seen—the shattered hands and feet, bodies ruined beyond repair, lives crushed in what were once peaceful villages among the world's most beautiful hills and valleys. She wonders whether he can sleep at night. The thought lies heavily behind her eyelids as she closes them.

How long must I push away the thought that Faiz might not return, she wonders. Fatima and Asma tell her she must believe he will come back, and until now she has been able to do it. But this day she has faced too many difficult truths, and she spends much of the night trying not to think of herself alone, of Faiz gone forever.

When she does sleep, she dreams a flood of salt water, an ocean of tears, threatens to engulf her and she has only her chadr to keep it away.

NUSRAT / NAJMAH
Peshawar, Pakistan

20

The next evening, after the kitchen is cleaned, Husna goes to her room for the night and Najmah sits on her bed working out math problems on a small wooden slate. Nusrat sets a kerosene lamp down on a small table in the garden beside the persimmon tree and pulls a cot from the kitchen stoop to an open spot between the tree and the garden wall. The sky is clear and the stars shimmer like diamonds stitched to a black velvet curtain. A heavy rain has washed the stink of dust and diesel from the air, but now the acrid smoke from wood- and dung-fueled fires drifts from the refugee camps.

Nusrat lies back on the cot and wraps her shawl tightly around her. The storm has brought chilled air from the mountains. She watches the stars rise, and once again wonders whether Faiz watches them too, whether he's safe and warm.

"I wish," Nusrat says, "that I had done what you wanted. I wish I'd conceived a child before you left. Perhaps you would have been more reluctant to take chances with your life if you had known you had a son or daughter to come home to."

The night before Faiz left to set up his first clinic in the South, he and Nusrat lay together looking at the sky on this same cot in the courtyard of the little house near the refugee camps.

"Will you think of me often?" he asked.

"You know I will," she said. It was a warm summer night, and the stars shimmered in a softer way than they did this night, with the haze of the day's heat making them waver.

"If you come out here every evening and look up at the stars, they will tell you where I am and that I am safe," he said.

And so every night she lies in the garden and looks up at the sky. Although she has never actually heard his voice as she watches, she has sensed that he looks at the very same stars and thinks of her.

But this night the stars and planets send back to

her nothing but cold, brilliant light and silence. They do not look like kindly messengers from her love. She thinks of the Pashtu saying that the stars are holes in the sky through which people in heaven look back on those who still love them. Tonight, she thinks, they look like fire, rock, and ice—elemental, impersonal. In that second she knows Faiz will not come back.

A sob tears itself from her deepest part, and she realizes even as it seems the world is ending that she has known for some time. She looks through the bare branches of the persimmon tree and the dark truth shines there with a blinding fierceness that she thinks very well might kill her.

/

The moment Bibi Nusrat refuses to allow Uncle into her garden, I am sure I can trust her. I've never known there were Muslims who had yellow hair, but she is a true Muslim. She is kind and she wants to take care of me the way my mother did. Mada-jan would be happy to have Bibi Nusrat looking after me.

When Uncle said that Baba-jan is dead, it struck my heart like a knife. But I will not believe him. I'm sure it's a trick. Uncle wants to grab our farm so that when we come back to Kunduz it will be too late for us to build a house and plant crops where he will already have planted his poppies. But I won't allow that to happen. I will get back to Golestan before he does, even if I have to go alone.

Bibi Nusrat is right: we must not speak to Haroon about finding Baba-Jan and Nur. I am quite certain the malek will feel obliged to send me back to Kunduz with Uncle.

I have a desperate urge to leave—right at this very moment. I want to walk home, although I know I will not make it alone. But if I stay here and no one knows where I am, how will Baba-jan and Nur find me?

The next morning Nusrat and I sit at the table eating naan and drinking tea. Her eyes are glazed and she looks as if she's spent the night crying. She seems not even to notice I am here. Just as I think this thought, she guesses what is in my mind.

"God will help us to find out about your father and brother," she says.

"But how?" I ask. "When?"

"I don't know, but believing in it will give us patience. Let's wait and see what happens. I will think about it and we'll talk about it. We will find a way, in sh'Allah!"

When I ask her what is the difference between Allah and the God of her childhood, she says, "They

are the same. I don't believe God cares by which language we name Him." I think she is right.

We decide I must not go into the bazaar for now,
except under a burqa, and only with Bibi Nusrat ac-
companying me. She is afraid Uncle might try to kid-
nap me. She has told Husna not to tell anyone that I
am staying with her. I don't know if I can trust that
sour-faced one. But once again, I have no choice.

Even when I am in the garden with the other students or just sitting in the sunshine, I cover my head.
This is my idea, because I know how clever Uncle is.
He may have spies watching Bibi Nusrat's house and
garden.

Bibi Nusrat is very sad. Several times I have seen
her lying at night under the stars on the cot, talking
to her husband and crying.

One night I go out to keep her company. I hesitate because I don't want to intrude on her. But I am
missing my Mada-jan and Baba-jan and my heart's
two brothers and all that was familiar and comfortable in my world before. I am too sad, knowing that
it will never again be as it once was. As I stand hesi-
tating behind where Bibi Nusrat lies on the cot in the
garden, a streak of silver flashes overhead in a perfect
arc that strikes terror into my heart.

Bibi Nusrat hears me gasp and sits up, turning

in my direction. The night before the death of my mother and Habib flashes before me, and I don't even see Bibi Nusrat in the golden light of the kerosene lamp.

"What is it?" she asks. But I cannot find my voice for several seconds.

"That sword," I whisper then, my voice faint and shaking. "I know it means something evil will happen. Someone will die!" Bibi Nusrat reaches for me and pulls me down on the cot beside her. Tears still glisten on her cheeks and she wraps her body-warmed pattu shawl around us both. This time I do not try to push her away. I'm shaking in every part of my body.

"That wasn't a sword," says Bibi Nusrat, her voice husky from crying. "It was a meteor, a piece of rock and ice broken from a comet hurtling through the sky." I swing my head and swivel my shoulders. I want to run and hide. But she holds on to me and there is nowhere to hide. Surely now they are shooting the stars from the sky!

I tell Bibi Nusrat about the hundreds and thousands of shining swords in the sky that night. "They flew in every direction all over the sky! When the sword appears in the sky, you know you'll draw your last breath!"

"No, Najmah," says Bibi Nusrat, turning me toward her on the cot so that I can see her face in the lantern's light. "What you saw that night was a meteor storm—something that happens rarely. You're a shepherd—you must have seen thousands of meteors cross the sky. It's a miracle of nature—not an omen of death!"

"After that night, when I went home I found the swords were right: I saw my Mada-jan and Habib die!" I am so frightened and filled with grief that I can hardly breathe.

"The swords are a made-up story to explain meteors," says Bibi Nusrat, her voice soothing. "They're not real. Meteors are ice and stone—they're real. Those who wanted people to obey them invented the stories to frighten everyone—that's where the myth comes from. But it isn't real."

"They're evil," I say again. My body feels used up and I slump against Bibi Nusrat, who holds me and rocks me back and forth.

"Listen," says Bibi Nusrat after a few moments. "In the holy city of Mecca is Islam's holiest place, in the center of which is the Ka'aba, which contains the Black Stone. You've heard of it."

I nod. Every Muslim child knows about the Ka'aba and the holy Black Stone. Every devout Muslim must make a pilgrimage to the Ka'aba at least once in a lifetime.

"The Black Stone fell from heaven at the feet of Ibrahim, and he put it into the Ka'aba. Many believe that what is in the holy shrine was part of a meteorite that fell from the sky right there in Mecca. That is quite possible. How can it be evil if it's part of the world's holiest shrine?" Somehow her words comfort me.

"Truly?" I ask, and lean back to look into her face again. Its curves are soft and round in the lamplight.

"Truly," Bibi Nusrat replies. We sit on the cot wrapped together in Bibi Nusrat's warm pattu shawl, each of us in our private world of grief.

Above us the sky is just as it always has been, alive with ancient figures that grow brighter, then dimmer as the night passes. Bibi Nusrat points out some stars and names them. They are stars I know by other names. I show her al-Qutb, the star around which the others move. "Polaris," she says. I tell her that al-Qutb is like the hub of a wheel, and she nods in recognition.

"My father taught me to bring the sheep and goats home safely through mountain pastures by making a fist and lining up the second knuckle with al-Qutb," I tell her. "It's the most constant star, and I'm never lost knowing it's there."

Bibi Nusrat hugs me to her. "Then you must

know precisely where you are now," she says. She's right. I am learning to see the sky differently.

All my life I have been looking at the night sky. To me it was something that was always there, like the grass underfoot or the water in the Baba Darya. It was the background for the stories that Baba-jan and Mada-jan told about the animals and the heroes and warriors and ancient kings that they and our ancestors and our ancestors' ancestors identified among the stars. Bibi Nusrat has taught me that the sky is endless space and time, and it makes my imagination do cartwheels trying to grasp what that might look like. I feel as unimportant as a speck of dust in it. After what's happened to my family, this is a comforting thought.

21

*L*ate in December, Wali and Ahmed leave
Peshawar with their family to return to Faisabad in
the Northeast. No new students come to the Persimmon Tree School. The only students who remain are
Najmah, Mansoora, and Amina. The winter weather
has turned bitter, and Nusrat moves them inside before the gas fire in the salon at the front of the house.

The government of Hamid Karzai takes its seat
in Kabul, and people feel optimistic, although the
fighting continues fiercely, first in one place, then in
another. In the South long skirmishes continue in
and around the city of Kandahar. To the north of Pe-

shawar guerrilla warfare is fierce among the hills of Tora Bora. But with the Taliban in retreat, people continue to return to their ruined farms in a state of euphoria. Even some of the refugees who have been in Peshawar for twenty years or more go home. The Americans will rebuild their houses, they say. So even if nothing is left, it's worth going home. No refugees come to Peshawar these days. The traffic goes in the opposite direction.

Nusrat cannot imagine not keeping the school open. Where would her students go? What would become of Mansoora's dream of becoming a teacher in her village in Paktia in eastern Afghanistan? Where would Najmah and Amina learn?

And without the school Nusrat's days would be far too long for her new circumstances. She would be alone with nothing to think about except every situation that will be different from now on because Faiz will not come home to her. She thinks of her family in Watertown and is jolted by the thought of telling them Faiz is gone. She thinks of New York and tries to imagine the skyline without the Twin Towers, the park without Faiz to walk beside her. She thinks of every place they have ever been, every dream they have ever dreamed together, and has to reimagine it all because Faiz is gone.

Worst of all, free time would leave her pondering

what might have happened to him, which one of the terrible rumors from Mazar-i-Sharif might be true.

She knows he is dead as surely as she knows that the almond trees will blossom in the spring. She no longer fools herself. If Faiz were still alive, he would have gotten word to her long before now. Even if he had been taken prisoner. But the Taliban holds no prisoners now that they are on the run. They kill their enemies. The bazaar is alive with women looking for sons and brothers and husbands who have disappeared in the fighting. Eventually most of them either find their relatives or learn where they died. But many do not, and, like Nusrat, these are the most desperate for news—even for bad news.

Nusrat still listens for the bell at the gate. But now it's not because she expects Faiz to walk into the garden. She begins to wish someone with news of what happened to him would ring the bell. It will be terrible, she knows—the pain will be excruciating. But nothing can be more terrible than not knowing. What she prays for now is that he did not suffer.

One cold winter night Nusrat lies on the cot in the courtyard watching the stars, wrapped in her shawl and a heavy quilt against the cold. Although she refuses to pretend that Faiz is still alive, who is to say he can't still talk to her through the stars?

When she sleeps that night she has the first

dream she's had since the night she dreamed of the ocean of tears. In this dream Nusrat is floating happily in the darkness of space. She feels light and at peace, and in every direction the stars shine in brilliant points. In the distance she sees two spots of pulsing, soft light. Nusrat focuses on them, and they become familiar shapes.

First Margaret floats into view, her hair spread out around her head, a blue gown around her legs. Her fingers extend toward Nusrat, who reaches for her sister. Nusrat's heart is filled with happiness to see her again after so many years. Their fingertips touch lightly and Margaret smiles. Nusrat stretches to hold on to her sister, but she floats away, out of sight.

The second figure is Faiz. This time Nusrat knows what to expect. She knows she will have to let him go. His eyes soften when he sees her, and he tilts his head to one side. Nusrat cannot speak, but she smiles at Faiz and mouths the words "I love you." Their fingertips brush each other before Faiz follows Margaret to drift among the stars.

When she awakens, Nusrat feels peace settling over the raw center of pain in her chest.

Najmah and Mansoora beg Nusrat to teach them English. Mansoora thinks that if her village can speak English they can make things that people in America and Europe will want. "We can listen to the BBC in English," she says. "We will know more about the world!" Najmah simply wants to learn everything there is to know.

And so the lessons in English begin. Mansoora, Najmah, and Amina are quick to learn. Nusrat gives them ten new vocabulary words every day. In the evenings Najmah asks for more.

"Walk with me," says Najmah in English one afternoon after the others have left and Nusrat is in the kitchen.

"But it's very cold," says Nusrat.

"Inside the house!" says Najmah. Bemused, Nusrat covers the bowl of dough she's been kneading and follows Najmah through the kitchen.

"Mez," says Najmah, laying her hand on the wooden table.

"Table," says Nusrat, and Najmah writes it down, showing it to Nusrat, who corrects the spelling. They continue this way through the house, naming everything in sight. Najmah's eyes twinkle, and she laughs with pleasure with each new word. She knows how to say and write every item of furniture, clothing, and food. Before long she can tell time and speaks in sentences. Nusrat delights in this girl, who has been so hurt by life at such a young age. Najmah gives Nusrat hope.

One day Nusrat and Najmah walk to the end of the street and engage Basharat to take them to University Town to visit Fatima, Asma, Sultan, and Jamshed.

Sultan greets them at the gate, and everyone takes turns embracing first Nusrat and then Najmah. Fatima runs her hand over Najmah's head. The hair is growing in, dark brown, soft and silky, curling around her face. Her skin glows with health and her eyes shine. Her confidence grows by the day. It's been almost a month since she came to Nusrat. Fatima clucks her tongue. They already treat her as if she were a family member.

"Such a beautiful girl," Fatima murmurs. "Why do you cut her hair so short?" Najmah ducks her head shyly. "Where have you been?" Fatima asks, turning to Nusrat. "I've been dying to see both of you!"

"We were here just three days ago," says Nusrat, laughing gently. Asma bends to hug Najmah, and when she straightens, Nusrat thinks she sees grief in her sister-in-law's eyes.

Jamshed is happy to see Najmah. The first time she came, he peered at her shyly from behind the door before coming out to watch and listen, and then committing himself to making a new friend. When she pushed back her burqa he stared at her hair, which still stuck out all over her head in bristles. Asma began to scold him for being rude, but Najmah had rubbed her hand over her stubbled head and laughed. So Jamshed laughed. The harder Najmah laughed, the harder Jamshed laughed. Even the adults laughed.

Nusrat has difficulty concentrating while her mother-in-law is in the room. Fatima has stopped saying, "Last time we heard from Faiz . . ." She now begins most sentences with something like "After Faiz is back safe and sound . . ." Nusrat can't bear this, but neither can she bring herself to tell Fatima that her son is dead. Time seems to have stopped for Fatima when Faiz was still with her, and she will not go forward again until he comes back. Nusrat fears there is no hope for her mother-in-law once she knows her son is gone.

Over and over, Fatima tells stories from Asma and Faiz's childhood in Kabul, when the city was alive with orchards and university students and exquisite Persian gardens, a time when every breath of air bore the scent of pomegranates and roses, and women met with other mothers and their children in the parks to eat picnic lunches and watch the little ones run and tumble.

Nusrat distracts herself by watching Najmah and Jamshed play in the large entry hall beside the salon.

He is so like Faiz, Nusrat thinks, as he shows Najmah how to hold the cricket bat and claps when she hits a small foam ball in the right direction.

"You will be the first female star—like Sachin Tendulkar," Jamshed says. Tendulkar is an Indian player who is the idol of every boy in the cricket-playing world. Asma warns them not to hit the ball too hard indoors.

When Fatima kisses Nusrat and Najmah good night, she scolds her daughter-in-law again. "Don't stay away so long next time," she says and goes off to bed. Sultan excuses himself and says he has work to do.

"Let me know when you and Najmah are ready to go and I'll take you home in the car," he says, wiggling his fingers at them. Nusrat knows he wants to give her and Asma a chance to talk.

"Poor Ma," says Asma, after they hear Fatima close the door to her room. "Her mind seems to be in a different time and place. Have you noticed? It's as if she can't bear to face up to whatever has happened. This is so hard!" Nusrat nods and smiles slightly.

"Oh!" says Asma, putting one hand over her mouth. "I'm so sorry, sister! It's been harder on you than anyone! Forgive me. It's just that you've been so brave. I can't imagine—"

"It doesn't matter," says Nusrat. "It's been hard

on all of us. He isn't coming back, Asma. You know that." Asma nods her head silently, and a tear slips out of each of her eyes and rolls down her cheeks.

"It's so hard to be around Ma," Asma says. "Sometimes I listen to her and she infects me with hope. Listen to me—as if hope were a disease! Sometimes I want to shake her, and say, 'Ma! He's dead! You can't go on pretending!' But I'm afraid it would kill her. You know?" She wipes the tears away impatiently with the backs of her hands.

Nusrat leans forward and takes Asma's hands in her own. "I've been thinking about my parents," she says. "For them my converting to Islam was a little as if I'd died. They felt they'd lost me. They're getting older now, and I think I need to go back."

"But you can't leave us!" Asma says. "Ever since you came to us you've said we're your family now!"

Nusrat smiles softly at her. "You are my family," she says. "Nothing will ever change that. I've grown so much in the time I've been here. Now I know that the family that brought me into the world also is my family. And, I think, so is Najmah. I'd like to spend some time with my mother and father, to make peace with them. I was all they had, and it hurt them terribly to lose me. I want to take Najmah with me."

"But they don't accept your being Muslim," says

Asma. "Do you think they'll accept your raising a child by yourself—an Afghan child?"

"I don't think I need for them to accept me so much now that I accept myself," she says. "Islam showed me what I was already coming to believe: that science and mathematics do not so much explain the universe as describe it. And with all that we know, there is still plenty of room for magic and mystery. If I'd been open to it, Christianity might have taught me the same things."

Asma takes a deep breath. "I would miss you terribly if you were gone."

"I won't leave until I know what happened to Faiz," she says. "And I would always come back! But without a husband I'm afraid the Pakistani government wouldn't allow me to live here, much less run the school."

"You could stay with us," Asma says. Nusrat shakes her head.

"I can't live here without work. I have no money and I would have nothing to contribute. It's different for you. Your mother and Sultan and Jamshed need you. You'll probably go back to Kabul soon. I could take Najmah to New York and give her a good life there. I will always come back to see you and Jamshed and Sultan and your mother. You are my family and my culture of choice. The culture in which I grew up doesn't make me so unhappy now that I know what I believe in and what I value. I know who I love and why. My culture will always be with me, wherever I go."

/

One night I am in my room, drawing the planets on my wooden slate. In addition to my white chalk I have nine colored chalks, one for each of the planets. In class we have learned about our solar system, and Bibi Nusrat has asked us to name the planets and to draw them in their order from the nearest to the farthest from the sun. She teaches this in English, and so it is doubly difficult. But every day I understand more quickly!

I am drawing beautiful pictures of the planets against the black sky when there is a soft rap on my door.

"Come in," I say. Bibi Nusrat opens the door quietly.

"Najmah," she says, "I've been thinking . . ." I look up and move my colored chalks and other things so she can sit with me on the cot. "I've been thinking how different your life would be if you came with me to America. You're healthy, Khuda-ra-shukur, and now that you have enough to eat you're putting on some weight and your hair is growing. If you go back to Kunduz, you won't have enough to eat again and there will be no medicine, no doctors, and no schools."

"What you say may be true," I say. "But there are many things of value in Kunduz." Nusrat doesn't say anything, and I feel the need to tell her about the things I love most to convince her of the importance of returning home. "The sky is so close you can reach up and touch it with your hands. The grapes hang from the vines in such a way that they let you know the precise moment to pick them. There is nothing like watching the melons grow fat in the sun. And the sheep trust us and go wherever we lead them, and turn their lambs over to us. Where would I find that in America?"

"If you go to a good school in America, you could be a doctor or a teacher or a lawyer—you could be anything you want to be. Have you ever thought about that?"

I shake my head, and for a moment I can think of nothing to say that will compare with what she offers.

"For hundreds of years my people have lived a good and simple life in hills that are more beautiful than anywhere on Earth," I say at last, for this is the truth. "I think always of the wind on my face and the smell of grass, the gentle sounds of the animals. I cannot imagine living anywhere else." My voice leaves me then for the first time since I came here to this kindest of women.

"I want you to think about coming to live with me in America. You don't need to tell me immediately. But will you think about it?" Bibi Nusrat asks. She waits for a moment. "We'll talk more about it when you're ready."

She has had so much pain. I do not want to give her more, so I nod yes, to say that I will think about it. Living anywhere but in Kunduz is unimaginable to me.

NAJMAH / NUSRAT
Peshawar, Pakistan

22

One night Bibi Nusrat is in the front room at her desk, writing letters. I am in my room writing sentences in English on my wooden slate when there is a pounding at the front door that rattles every window in the house. I hear footsteps and a man speaking angrily, and I know it is Uncle. My heart leaps into my mouth. I know Bibi Nusrat will not tell him I am here. But what if he forces his way inside? I turn out the light in my room and slip out into the hallway to listen. I hear the malek Haroon say, "Baghlani Saheb says he knows his niece is staying here with you. Someone who has seen her enter and leave this house has told him."

There is a silence of several seconds. And then Bibi Nusrat says, "There was a girl here looking for work. She said her family came from the city. She did not look like a country girl. But I already have a servant. I sent her to Dr. Naveed down the road. I heard he was looking for someone."

My heart, which has been learning to feel comfortable and safe, begins to beat so wildly I fear it will give me away as I hide in the hallway, straining to hear every word. It is true that a girl was here and that Bibi Nusrat sent her to Dr. Naveed. But Uncle is angry. Someone has told him I am here. With the Taliban hiding everywhere and so many people spying on neighbors and even family members, it's difficult to keep secrets. I wonder whether it might have been Bibi Nusrat's sour old servant. I look around to see where I might hide if Uncle forces his way into the house. No one speaks for several seconds and time stands still.

After I hear the front door close, Bibi Nusrat comes quickly down the hall, light on her feet, her daman rustling softly, to find me hiding in the cupboard in her bedroom, my face hidden among her shawls. She doesn't try to get me to come out. Instead she crawls in beside me and draws the door almost shut so a little light filters in and we can just see each other in outline.

"It has been some weeks since your uncle was here looking for you," Bibi Nusrat whispers softly. "I had begun to wonder whether I only imagined his first visit. But sometimes I feel anxiety tugging at my heart, and I know he is all too real."

"Yes," I say, nodding in agreement. "Uncle is real—not a sword in the sky but ice and rock, like a meteor." Bibi Nusrat laughs softly and hugs me against her. I hug her back.

"I did not invite him and Haroon inside," she says. In my mind's eye I see her stand to one side in the doorway so that they can see into the empty living room. In my mind's picture Bibi Nusrat is very calm, and after a moment she says good night and shuts the door softly. "Perhaps your uncle believed me," she says.

I shake my head. "He knows I'm here. I don't know how he knows—but I'm sure he does. It won't be long before he comes back—perhaps with a Pashtun talib—to search your house. I don't think it's safe for me to stay."

We say nothing for a few moments, both of us thinking. We hear a kind of scraping sound at the side of the house, and I feel the skin between my shoulder blades rise into bumps. I imagine the worst.

"What if they break in through the window?" I whisper so softly I'm not sure Bibi Nusrat hears me. She says nothing, and I feel her shake against me. It frightens me to think she's so scared that she trembles. But she sucks a little air in through her nose, and I realize she's laughing!

"Can't you see him?" she whispers against my hair. I can feel her breath on my ear. "He's so fat—he'll get stuck in those little windows." Suddenly the image of Uncle's head and his very serious turban in the room, and his wide bottom and little feet wiggling outside behind him, is too much to bear. We both laugh so hard that Bibi Nusrat pulls the cupboard door shut in case anyone is listening outside the windows. It feels so good to laugh! It feels as if the world might very well go on.

We awaken some hours later, still inside the cupboard. Bibi Nusrat tells me to stay there while she tiptoes across the room and looks out the window. She lights the lantern. Through the space under the cupboard door I see the light move as she walks from room to room. When she returns, she sets down the lantern and opens the door to the cupboard.

"We may as well sleep the rest of the night in our beds," she says. "No one is here but Husna and us. I've let the chickens out into the garden, and they will let us know if there are any intruders."

When I get into bed and close my eyes, I smell the sun-burnt grass and hear the breeze whispering through the cedars on Koh-i-Dil, the steady *chuff-chuff-chuff* of the sheep cropping the dry grass, and my heart feels a pain in its center. I think of Nur and how he teased me, even on the last morning we slept in the same house with no thought that this would be our family's last day together. Nur led me on so many chases to childish fear and anger. But even then I knew he would have laid down his life for me. I see his eyes the color of cedar bark and his bow-shaped lips with laughter always playing at their corners, his square hands that threw rocks very far to make the sheep go where he wanted them to go, but were tender with helping the ewes birth their lambs. How will he find me if I cannot let it be known in the refugee camps that I am here? How can I let him know without having Uncle force me to go back to Golestan with him?

I promised Bibi Nusrat that I will think about going with her to America. It makes sense for so many reasons, but not in my heart. There I cannot think of anything but returning to the hills of Kunduz.

In the cupboard at the foot of my cot lie the laundered and neatly folded derishi and the turban that Akhtar gave me. I think of putting them on and becoming Shaheed once again, and slipping out to find my people in the Shahnawaz refugee camp.

/

Nusrat goes to her own room and lies in the dark, still dressed. She stares up at the ceiling, where Faiz had pasted small iridescent plastic stars for her to contemplate before she sleeps. A tear trickles from the corner of her eye and falls into her ear. She wipes angrily at her face. How could he leave her in this place, where a man like Mohiuddin Baghlani menaces her? Her heart hurts, and another tear pools in the small well between her eye and nose.

She gets up before dawn without sleeping and splashes cold water on her face and says her morning prayers. She goes to the kitchen quietly and lights the stove and fills the kettle. Najmah comes into the kitchen rubbing at her tired eyes and sits at the large wooden table.

"Did you sleep?" asks Nusrat, and Najmah shakes her head. "Tea will be ready in just a moment."

"Did you sleep?" Najmah asks. Nusrat smiles and shakes her head.

"We have both had so many difficult things to think about," says Nusrat. "I can't stay here, and yet I can't bear to leave."

"Surely you can stay with Fatima-jan and Khala Asma?" Najmah asks.

"It's not that," says Nusrat. "I need to live where I can work. The Pakistani government wouldn't give me a visa to stay here on my own. I've thought of going back to America to teach in New York. You could come with me and go to the International School. The students come from all over the world. I think you would like that."

"Can you see the stars in New York?" Najmah asks after a moment's silence.

"Yes," says Nusrat, "you can see the stars in New York. The city lights are bright, so the stars seem dim. But there are many other things to see in New York."

"But you cannot see the mountains," says Najmah.

"In New York there are buildings as tall as mountains," Nusrat says, and thinks of the Twin Towers, which were as tall as mountains.

"My entire life I have lived in the shadow of the Hindu Kush," says Najmah. "My heart would cry if I could not see the mountains every day. And I would not know where I was if I could not see al-Qutb, the star that never moves."

"But you would have so many other things," says Nusrat, "—school, friends, family. You will have enough to eat and good care and a good education. If you stay here your life will be very difficult. You cannot go back to Kunduz alone. Your uncle would take your father's land and you would have nothing."

"He will take the land if I stay here," says Najmah. "That is why I must find my Baba-jan and Nur." Najmah folds her arms in front of her and sets her jaw in a way that has become familiar to Nusrat. "You must promise to stay with me until I find them!" she says fiercely. "Otherwise I don't know what I will do."

"So many people never find what has become of their loved ones," says Nusrat gently. But her words are like a slap. Najmah takes a deep breath and hugs herself.

"I know," she says finally. "But I must try to find out. And whether they are alive or dead, I must find a way to go back."

"Just as I must find out what happened to my husband," says Nusrat. "I promised that I will help look for your family. I will help in any way that I can." But Nusrat's heart feels heavy, and she has no idea how they will go about finding Najmah's father and brother.

They go through the rest of the morning getting ready for class and making lunch, feeling hollow with sleeplessness and uncertainty, until Mansoora and Amina arrive. There is much to do, as Husna has taken the day to go to Nowshera to visit her sister.

Amina and Mansoora are talkative and excited as usual, and Nusrat's spirit lifts slightly. Then, in the middle of the English lesson, a strange and miraculous thing happens. It is a very cold day and the wind blows gusts of dust and plastic bags into swirls outside the windows, but they are cozy sitting on the floor before the gas fire. Nusrat sits on a hassock and tells them about English words that sound the same but have different meanings.

When she hears the bell jangle at the gate, she forgets for a moment that Husna is not there, and ignores it until it jangles more insistently. She leaves them writing words on their wooden slates and goes out to see who is there.

Standing with Haroon is what Nusrat thinks at first is a ghost. Covered from head to toe in a heavy layer of dust is a boy who looks almost exactly like Najmah—right down to the surmeh-rimmed eyes and the too-large chappals. He is taller than Najmah and not so fine-boned. His shoulders are broad and his hands are thick. Nusrat thinks surely her mind is playing tricks on her.

"I have another student for you," says Haroon after they exchange greetings. The boy stands very still with his eyes level and his teeth clamped on the edge of a striped gray turban. He holds his shoulders straight and square.

"Well, Haroon, as usual your timing is perfect. Will you join us for a meal?" Nusrat asks. Haroon puts his hand over his heart and thanks Nusrat but says he must get back to the camp. His manner is so contrite and his departure so hasty that she realizes this child also is most likely in need of a place to stay. She laughs, thanking Haroon's retreating back, and invites the boy into the garden.

Najmah and Mansoora are in the kitchen setting plates and glasses on the table when Nusrat comes in with her new student. Mansoora and Amina stare at the dust-covered newcomer, and when Najmah looks up, there is a loud crash as the stack of plates in her hands falls to the floor and shatters.

23

I run to Nur and throw my arms around him. His face crumples like a burning piece of paper when he sees me, and we stand face-to-face staring at each other for a long time. I am not aware of anything in the world except that Nur is here at last.

I stand back and drink him in like someone caught in the desert for days with no water. He seems much as I must have seemed when I came to Bibi Nusrat: mute, staring, and frightened. Tears make little muddy rivers through the dust on his cheeks and his mouth is open wide, with no sound coming out.

"Baba-jan?" I ask before we even say hello. He

says nothing, but continues staring with his mouth open and tears running down his face. Suddenly I realize that the things Nur and I have seen these past three months make us many ages older because the world we knew has come to an end.

Nusrat insists on feeding us. She knows who Nur is without having to ask. "Just eat something and we will leave you alone to talk," she says, bustling about the kitchen and setting a place for Nur at the table. She leads him to the sink to wash his hands and face. He sits in a chair near the center of the table, looking dazed and still not speaking, with me across from him. Bibi Nusrat, Amina, and Mansoora take their food to the front room and eat by the fire.

I am glad the pinch-faced one is not here to begrudge Nur the mounds of food he eats. It's as if he has never eaten in his life. He is very thin. His neck is all sinew, like a goat's, and his ears stick out from under his turban; his hands and feet and shoulders are larger than I remember; and he is much taller than I am, although we were almost even just a short time ago.

I finish eating long before Nur does, and I watch silently as he has a second heaped plateful of lentils and rice and chicken. After lunch Bibi Nusrat leads Nur and me into the front room and seats Amina and Mansoora at the kitchen table to work on their lessons. She brings us green tea flavored with cardamom. I remember when I first came to Bibi Nusrat how this special treat gave me great pleasure, and now I have grown accustomed to drinking it every day. A glow of gratitude for Bibi Nusrat's kindness settles into my heart, and I thank her with my eyes as she moves about efficiently, making us comfortable in front of the gas fire.

"We'll work in the kitchen," Bibi Nusrat says softly, pulling the curtain across the arched entry into the salon as she leaves to give us privacy.

"Mada-jan . . ." I begin at the same time as Nur starts to speak with "Baba-jan . . ." We look at each other for a long time. It's the first Nur has spoken, and I am surprised at how deep his voice has grown.

"You talk first," I say quietly. "What I have to say is very hard." Tears brim in his eyes again and he nods.

"Baba-jan is dead," he says softly, his voice cracking. I knew he would say these words before they formed in his mouth. Why would he come here alone if our father were alive? Nur's voice is scratchy and soft, as though he has not spoken in a long time. I realize I have known what happened since long before he arrived here. It's as if our meeting has played out in my mind like a dream. I knew Nur would survive, despite the way the Pashtun talib leader treated him so roughly that first day. And I knew Baba-jan would not. Baba-jan was too kind. In the face of such evil and cruelty the gentle seldom survive.

"Go on," I say.

"They separated us not long after they took us from Golestan. They told the boys to stay behind the hill with a guard. They took Baba-jan and the other village men in their trucks. They tied their hands behind their backs and they drove off, over the hill, with the men crowded in the back like cattle. They didn't go far. Not long after, we heard gunshots—very close together, one after another—bang! Bang! Bang, bang, bang! It echoed through the hills, and it was difficult to say how many bullets they fired.

"But when they came and got us, none of the men from Golestan were in the trucks. We thought we would die next. They ordered us into the back of the trucks and we were sure they would take us to the same spot and shoot us, too. They took us a short distance away, where we saw the men of our village —nearly every grown man you and I have ever known—lying on the ground with their bodies over-lapping each other, with blood coming from bullet holes in their heads and bodies." He says their names slowly and separately, as if to remember them properly.

"Khalifa Daoud. Usman Khan. Mama Rahim.

Nasir e rangmal. Iqbal e najar. Baba-jan. You cannot imagine how this robbed our hearts of all hope. After we saw our fathers and uncles and other village men dead, we wanted them to kill us, too. But they made us dig a large hole and put their bodies inside and then cover them up." He takes a deep breath and looks up at me, his eyes holding a deep well of sorrow. He shakes his head as if he still has trouble believing what he saw.

"You and I are the only family we have left, Nur," I say quietly. I tell him about the birth of Habib, and the bombs falling, and everything that happened the day that he and I became orphans. When I have finished, Nur sits still, his head nodding slightly, and I know that he knew about Mada-jan and Habib, just as I had known about Baba-jan. Neither of us has any tears left to cry.

Bibi Nusrat sends Amina and Mansoora away early and comes to see if we need anything. We say no, but she brings us more tea, and then turns to leave the room.

"Please stay," Nur says. We tell her about Baba-jan and the other men in our village.

"Then you must agree," she says, looking from Nur's face to mine, "that you cannot go back to a village where you have no one to help you. Your uncle will take your land. Who would stop him from killing you and taking everything?" Nur and I look at each other.

"We have no choice but to return to Golestan," says Nur quietly. "Uncle or someone else surely will take our land if we don't go back. It was our father's last wish that we should keep our farm from the hands of the Taliban or Uncle. It is where our father's father and his father's father and so many generations before them made their lives, and it is our duty to make our life there and the lives of our children and our children's children. This is a matter of the greatest honor to us. We must do everything to obey our father's wishes, no matter what the cost. If we do not, we may as well die."

"But you surely *will* die!" says Bibi Nusrat, sinking down into a chair beside me and across from Nur. She raises her hands and covers her mouth. "Two children can't walk across the mountains for so many days in winter. There is still fighting. There are land mines. There are bandits!" She looks very frightened, and her fear for us touches me. Nur and I don't know what to do or say. I put my hand on her shoulder, and she covers it with her hand.

"We can't stay here," says Bibi Nusrat, drawing a deep breath. She stands up abruptly, knocking her chair to the floor with a clatter, as if she's just thought of the danger we're in. "Your uncle will soon learn that Nur is here, and he'll come back—I'm certain of it. He might even come tonight. We should go to University Town and stay with Khala Asma and Sultan. We must go now. Najmah, please pack your things. I'll go and fetch Basharat to take us. We'll be safer with Asma and Sultan."

I have grown used to feeling safe with Bibi Nusrat, and my heart feels leaden when I realize that Nur and I are in danger again, and because of us, Bibi Nusrat is also in danger. Nur and I go to my room while I gather my few belongings.

Nur arrived with nothing—he has no money, no clothes other than those he wears, no blanket, no weapons. He sits on the edge of my bed as I gather together my clothes and zip them into the cloth suitcase in my cupboard. There is just room for my wooden slate and my chalks, which I wrap in a towel. Nur's head nods, and he can barely hold his eyes open as he watches me pack.

We hear the bells of the tonga horses at the back gate, and Nur is wide awake again. He takes my suitcase and hands it to Basharat, who puts it under the seat. Bibi Nusrat goes inside to get warmer shawls for us all, since the weather has grown colder. In the tonga Nur falls asleep, his head rolling and bobbing sharply as the wheels bounce over ruts and holes in the road.

We arrive at Khala Asma's house just before tea-time. She comes to greet us in the courtyard, her face happy with a look of surprise. She is wrapped in a warm shawl, and puffs of steam flow from her mouth as she speaks. I introduce her to Nur, and she shakes his hand warmly as Bibi Nusrat tells Basharat that Sultan will take us back home. Basharat walks back toward the tonga, and Bibi Nusrat calls him back. She speaks quietly to him and I overhear her say, "You must not tell anyone you've brought us here, especially not Haroon." Basharat touches his forehead and bows deeply as he says goodbye again, his eyes flickering among our faces.

"Come into the kitchen where it's warm," Khala Asma says. "I'm just going in to light the gas fire so we can have tea in the salon." In the kitchen Khala Asma and Fatima kiss me and Bibi Nusrat. Fatima is very happy to see us, as always, but Khala Asma looks worried, as if she senses the danger we're in.

Jamshed is excited to see us. At first he stares at Nur without speaking, taking in my brother's turban and the dust that still covers him.

"Are you mujahideen?" Jamshed asks, his eyes widening. Nur looks at me and then at Bibi Nusrat and nods his head. "Where is your gun?" Jamshed asks, his voice rising with excitement. "Have you shot anyone?"

"Jamshed!" Khala Asma says, giving him a sharp look.

"Sorry," says Jamshed. Nur looks uncomfortable.

"Why don't you take Nur to the back bedroom?" Khala Asma suggests. "He can have a hot bath, and we'll find him something clean to wear." She goes to the laundry cupboard and comes back with a shirt and trousers and sweater that look to be about Nur's size.

"These belonged to Faiz when he was a student," she says. "I was keeping them for Jamshed. They'll fit Nur." Jamshed leads the way down the hallway and Nur follows. Bibi Nusrat takes the clothes to the tashnab and lights the gas heater in the wall. I come to watch Nur's expression.

Nur watches carefully, with interest, although his shoulders stoop with exhaustion. He takes off his turban, and even his hair, which is long and unkempt, is covered in grayish dust. His face and hands are starkly pale from having washed them before his dinner. I stand close to him in the hallway while his bath water runs, and he smells of wood smoke and lamb fat and dust.

When he emerges from the tashnab his skin is pink and clear. He looks as if the bath has revived him. Faiz's clothing fits him surprisingly well. Nusrat asks if he wants to sleep, and he says he'd rather wait and sleep when everyone else goes to bed.

When Sultan arrives from the city, we move to Khala Asma's salon, which is furnished with beautiful Persian rugs and soft velvet sofas and chairs. Sultan pours himself a whiskey and joins us as we sip tea in fine china cups. Nur holds his as if it will break in his large fingers.

Everyone is careful not to question Nur too closely, but he is eager to talk, and Jamshed sits on the floor staring up into my brother's face as Nur tells how he escaped by a mountain path to the north of Jalalabad when his commander was wounded.

"The men in our group had been together for three months," he says. "Everyone just left the leader there with a bullet hole in his shoulder. Each of us ran in a different direction—some went up over the hill, straight for Jalalabad, others scattered toward where they thought they might find their families or back toward their farms.

"We had grown to know each other well because we saved each other's lives and watched many others just like us die. And yet we didn't speak when the time came to go. We did not say goodbye. We'll never see each other again. Not one of them was a real talib—they had been taken from their villages just as I had been. The Taliban began to be disorganized as the mujahideen won more battles, and they did not take as much care about keeping us, and so we were able to leave."

Nur made his way to Torkhum much as I had done; only his ride to Peshawar was in a car filled with foreigners. The automobile was heated and had soft seats. It was clean and smelled of perfume, Nur said. "I did not know that I would survive until I saw the mujahideen with flowers in their gun barrels. Then I knew the Taliban was losing this war."

As he talks, I think of things I've left out of my story. It feels urgent that I tell him every detail of what's happened to me since I saw him last—about Uncle looking for me and telling Bibi Nusrat that Baba-jan and he were dead, about sleeping in the fruit cart, and about my studies at Bibi Nusrat's, the things I've learned about stars.

Sultan sits quietly listening to my brother talk until Nur's eyes look heavy again. Nur excuses himself and goes to his room in the back of the house. In University Town the electricity stays on until late most nights, and kerosene lamps aren't necessary.

A little while later Bibi Nusrat hugs me and sends me off to sleep in the room she and I will share. It's early, but I assume she wants to talk to Sultan and Asma about her plans. I lie in bed, staring at the ceiling, until Bibi Nusrat comes in to sleep much later, sometime in the middle of the night. I pretend I'm sleeping because I don't want to talk to her. I don't want to hear her say again how dangerous it is for Nur and me to travel to Kunduz. I don't want to have to tell her again that I cannot go with her to New York. I don't fall asleep until she lies down quietly beside me, but somehow I manage to sleep until morning.

The next day Sultan drives Bibi Nusrat to her house in time to greet Mansoora and Amina. She tells them she will have to cancel their lessons for a few days.

She returns and tells us the sour-faced servant has not returned from Nowshera as she agreed she would. Bibi Nusrat went into the servant's quarters to see if there was anything that might tell why Husna was so late coming back. The room was empty of everything, including things that belonged to Husna and things that did not. I wonder whether Husna left because she was afraid she'd be found out for telling Haroon and Uncle that I had come to live in Bibi Nusrat's house. Or perhaps she could not bear Bibi Nusrat's generosity to other people any longer. Perhaps Husna thought she should be the only beneficiary. I do not know.

Nur sleeps almost around the clock. It's teatime

when he stumbles down the hallway and into the kitchen, where Khala Asma, Bibi Nusrat, the ayah Maha, and I make tea and set out dishes of cake and cups and spoons.

Khala Asma tells us that Jamshed is having tea with his cricket mates.

When we have assembled in the beautiful formal sitting room Sultan is already settled in his armchair with a whiskey on the table, talking intently into the cordless telephone that he carries around the house with him. Nur and I hesitate in the doorway, not wanting to interrupt his conversation. But he motions us into the room and soon switches off the telephone.

When we are all seated, Khala Asma and Maha bring in the tea and set it on the table. Bibi Nusrat pours the tea, and the room seems unnaturally quiet. Sultan clears his throat.

"Nusrat tells me that you two intend to return to Kunduz—despite many dangers—to take control of your family's land," he says, addressing Nur and me. I say nothing and Nur nods his head. "You are aware that local tribesmen have set up roadblocks all along the roads." Sultan pauses, and Nur and I look at each other but say nothing.

"They take people out of their automobiles and shoot them and steal their cars and their belongings.

They're taking children from their parents and using them as farm labor and worse."

Nur watches Sultan, unblinking and silent. Sultan stares back, and finally Nur says, "Yes, we know about the danger. But we feel we have no choice. We will not go by road." To our surprise Sultan does not disagree.

"I understand," he says. "The airports are closed and very few airplanes are left to fly. So it's impossible to go any way other than overland. But it's a very dangerous and difficult walk, going cross-country." Nur nods his head again.

"I've just been talking to General Durrani," Sultan goes on. "His mujahideen in Kunduz Province remain loyal to him, even though he's left combat to join the government. He has agreed to send some of his men with us to Mazar-i-Sharif. Nusrat, Asma, and I will go there to see if we can find what happened to Dr. Faiz."

Nusrat sits quietly in her chair, her hands folded in her lap. Khala Asma's brow is furrowed.

"From Mazar-i-Sharif, General Durrani's men will take you on to Kunduz," Sultan says. "It will still be dangerous, but having them protect you is the safest way to go." When he finishes, Nur does not look at me. He stands before Sultan and takes his hand, his voice choked with emotion as he thanks him. Sultan takes Nur gently by the arms and embraces him.

"There is no need to thank me," Sultan says gently, his voice veiled with emotion. "We are all Afghans and we know what we must do."

Nur and I sit up and talk late into the night in the kitchen. Khala Asma and Maha bring us food and tea, but otherwise they leave us alone. We have so much to talk about—I want to ask him how we will cope with Uncle and how we will manage to build a house and start a new herd with no money.

At first we do not speak of these things. We spend our words on the time that we have been apart. No detail is too small: the fleas in the blankets that Nur slept in, the people from our village who died in addition to the older men like Baba-jan, the foreigners who told the commanders where to go after a battle, and how they walked through many nights with no food. So many terrible things.

"The Taliban are not finished yet," Nur tells me. "The foreigners have told the Taliban leaders to hide in the mountains until other fighters come from other countries. They speak Arabic and Urdu and some other languages. Some are from Africa. The leaders did not tell us any of these things directly, but we heard many words that were not meant for our ears. They thought we were stupid, and sometimes they were careless."

/

The next day Nusrat and Asma and Sultan make plans to go to Mazar-i-Sharif to see for themselves where Faiz last lived and worked. They send for Babar, the son of a neighbor who had seen Faiz in Kandahar before returning to Peshawar to care for his sick father. Babar tells them the names of several people who went to Mazar-i-Sharif with Faiz. Sultan sends someone to find the family of one of the men. But the family have not heard from their relative since he left Kandahar with the Amriki doctor. Sultan promises to call them if he hears any news, and they agree to do the same. They sound to Sultan as if they have given up hope.

Sultan drives his car to Nusrat's house and brings back clothes for her. He finds things exactly the way Nusrat had left them when she brought Nur and Najmah to University Town three days earlier. Sultan waits for General Durrani's men to contact him to say they're ready to accompany them to Mazar-i-Sharif and Kunduz.

Nusrat is restless in the house in University Town. She is accustomed to being busy, and the waiting distresses her. She paces in the salon and in her room and up and down the hallways. When the sun shines, she sits in the garden wrapped in warm shawls. She does not go out at night to look at the stars. Najmah and Nur spend their days talking in Nur's room.

One day Nur and Najmah come looking for Nusrat in the kitchen. They stand before her as she kneads bread in a wooden bowl that sits on the worn kitchen table. She looks up at them with a bemused little frown on her face.

"Bibi Nusrat, will you come and talk to us, please?" Najmah asks quietly. "Nur has something to tell you." Nusrat's heart pounds, and she drops the bread into the bowl and wipes her hand on the towel that's tied at her waist by the laces of her apron. She follows them without speaking to the doorway to Nur's room, and the three of them look at each other for a moment before Nur motions her inside to sit on his cot.

Nur and Najmah stand side-by-side on the worn red-and-brown kilim beside the cot facing Nusrat, their backs to the doorway.

"I was in Mazar-i-Sharif some time ago," Nur begins, "and I heard something about an Amriki doctor. Until just now I did not know he might have been your husband." Nusrat straightens her spine and nods, and Nur goes on. "There was an accidental bombing raid on the western edge of the city early in the fall. I don't know exactly when. A village was destroyed and many people were killed. People said a clinic there also was destroyed and several people died. We passed the village about a week later. There was nothing left of it. They said an Amriki doctor was killed in the bombing. I have no more information than that."

Nusrat continues nodding as Nur speaks. When he finishes, she sits quietly for a while, and then she stands and goes back to the kitchen, where she sits immobile on the stool beside the table and stares at the dough in the bread bowl. Nur and Najmah follow her into the kitchen, but they leave her to be alone with their words.

Sultan is in the city talking to people who might have news about the roads between Peshawar and Mazar-i-Sharif. Jamshed is in school. Fatima is unwell, and Nusrat goes to Asma, who sits beside her mother's bed. Fatima looks even more birdlike than usual. Her eyes are darker and brighter with fever. Her hair is loose and wild and white around her thin face, which is pale except for two small red patches over her cheekbones. When Fatima falls asleep with her eyes moving rapidly from side to side behind her eyelids, Nusrat takes Asma by the hand and leads her into the salon.

Maha brings them tea, and Nusrat tells Asma what Nur has said about the clinic in the western suburb of Mazar-i-Sharif. Asma listens to the news, searching her sister-in-law's face carefully. When Nusrat finishes speaking, Asma drops her face into her hands and takes a long deep breath.

"It's better to know," Asma says, and Nusrat agrees.

"This is the most likely thing to have happened," Nusrat says. "I believe the story Nur heard in Mazar-i-Sharif might have been the truth, although we may never know for certain. But I want now more than ever to go there to find out what there is to know." Asma nods without speaking. Tears flow down her face and she holds her stomach, rocking back and forth. Nusrat holds her sister-in-law in her arms and rocks with her.

They sit together for a while, and then Nusrat comes back to the kitchen to help Maha get dinner ready for when Jamshed and Sultan return. She knows Asma wants to be alone with the news of Faiz, that she will think about how to tell her husband and especially her son that Faiz will not come back to them.

There are few happy endings in Afghanistan these days. But there are good endings, with people doing what is true to their hearts, difficult things that spare dignity, painful things that are the right thing to do. These endings are inevitable for people who are true to themselves.

How can a woman named Help not return to America to make peace with her family? Perhaps she will return to Afghanistan to honor the name her husband gave her by building a school there.

And how can a girl named Star and a boy named Light not go back to their land in the shadow of a mountain named to honor their ancestors' hearts? For there is great value to lives lived in a village called Golestan, which means "beautiful garden."

Glossary

Note: Most of the words in this glossary are used by Dari-speaking people in Afghanistan. Dari is a language very similar to the Persian spoken in Iran. Many languages have influenced Dari, including Arabic, Hindi, Urdu, and English. Many of these words also are used in India, Pakistan, and countries of the Middle East.

Afghan—a person of Afghanistan
Afghani—currency of Afghanistan
Ah-salaam-aleikum—traditional Islamic greeting (Arabic; literally, God's peace with you)
Amriki—American
amrud—a white or pinkish, pear-like fruit known in English as guava
ayah—a female servant, often a maid who looks after children and does other household work
baba—father, or an elderly man (often used as a suffix to a name)
Baba-jan—Father dear

bacha—son or boy; often used affectionately to address a male child

Bibi—female term of respect and affection; a name

Bismillah ar-Rahman ar-Raheem—Beginning of prayer (Arabic; literally, in the name of God, the compassionate, the merciful)

bukri—goat

burqa—a traditional head-and-body-covering for Islamic women in Afghanistan and parts of Iran, India, and Pakistan. It consists of many yards of fabric gathered and stitched to a close-fitting cap. A latticed hole in front of the eyes allows limited vision

chadr—a plain piece of cloth about fifty inches square used as a head-and-upper-body-covering

chai—tea

chappals—open-toed leather sandals

daman—skirt

Dari—Persian language spoken in much of Afghanistan

dereshi—suit of clothes

djinn—a ghost or spirit made of fire that appears mainly at night; can be invisible or assume the shape of an animal

ghee—cooking oil (originally, clarified butter)

harakat—a social or political movement; often a political party

imam—the leader of prayer in a mosque

in sh'Allah—God willing (Arabic)

jan—heart; a term of endearment often affixed after a name or title

jor bash—Dari greeting (literally, may you be well)

Ka'aba—the holiest shrine of Islam in the city of Mecca, built by Abraham (who is known in Islam as Ibrahim)

khala—maternal aunt, usually preceding the person's name

khalifa—master (craftsman or teacher) or headman

khan—term of respect (formerly a royal title) that translates roughly as Mr. or sir, used particularly by Pashtuns

khanum—Mrs. or madam

kheer—a dessert made by boiling milk and rice, and flavored with honey, green cardamom, and almonds or pistachios

Khuda—God

Khuda-hafez—goodbye (Arabic; literally, God look after you)

Khuda-ra-shukur—thank God

mada—mother

Mada-jan—Mother dear

madrassa—a religious school for Muslims (Arabic: school)

malek—administrative manager

mama—maternal uncle

mande nabash—Dari greeting (literally, may you never be tired)

Masha' Allah—God's will

masjid—mosque

memsaheb—a polite term for a lady, particularly a foreigner (from Hindi and English—madam-saheb)

mez—table

muallem—teacher

mujahid—an Islamic warrior

mujahideen—name assumed by Afghans who fought first against the former Soviet Union and then against the Taliban

mullah—a religious leader

naan—unleavened bread baked in a mud oven

najar—carpenter

pakul—a woolen hat worn in northern areas, rolled up from the hem

Pashtu—language of Pashtun tribal groups

Pashtun—the tribal group that forms the ethnic majority of Afghanistan; traditionally from the East and South, they live all over Afghanistan (also known as Pathans)

Pashtun talib—religious fundamentalists who enforced the rigid code of the Taliban government that ruled Afghanistan 1996–2001

pattu—woolen shawl worn by men and women

pillau—rice dish usually cooked with meat or vegetables

Punjabi dereshi—suit of clothes in the style of Punjab province in eastern Pakistan; wide-legged trousers and a long-sleeved, loose-fitting tunic

purdah—a screen or curtain used for privacy; also the practice of separating women from men

qibla—a wall or marking on a wall to guide worshippers in facing toward the Holy Kaaba in Mecca for prayer

rangmal—a painter

Red Crescent—the world relief organization known in non-Muslim lands as the Red Cross

saheb—a term of respect (male), particularly for a foreigner of rank

saheba—term of respect usually for a foreigner (female)

shahab—meteorite or shooting star

Shahada—profession of faith in one God and one Prophet; the first pillar of Islam

shalwar kameez—a suit of clothing that consists of a long-sleeved, knee-length, loose tunic worn over a pair of flowing trousers usually tapered into an embroidered cuff at the ankle. The shalwar kameez originally came from Pakistan's Punjab province and is sometimes called "punjabi" in Afghanistan

sulaiman—a type of small raisin

surmeh—oily black substance used to outline the eyes and protect them from disease

Tajik—Persian-speaking people ethnically related to the people of Tajikistan to the north of Afghanistan; in northern Afghanistan, many are herders and small farmers; they often work in government positions

talib—seeker (Arabic)

Taliban—Afghan fundamentalist Muslims known for their harsh rule of Afghanistan from 1996 to 2001, and for their support of the terrorist al-Qaeda group led by Osama bin Laden

tashnab—bathroom

tonga—a small carriage or large cart drawn by one or two horses, usually made of wood

toshak—large pillow or small mattress made of carpet and woven backing

Waleikum-ah-salaam—and God's peace with you (Arabic), in response to a greeting

GOFISH

questions for the author

SUZANNE FISHER STAPLES

What did you want to be when you grew up?
A veterinarian or a writer.

When did you realize you wanted to be a writer?
About the same time I realized I wanted to be a veterinarian. I was probably three or four, and the only thing I loved as much as stories was animals.

What's your first childhood memory?
I remember my father coming home from work (I was 2 ½) and throwing me up in the air and catching me. It was the day we moved into the first house my parents owned in Jermyn, Pennsylvania.

What's your most embarrassing childhood memory?
I can't bear to tell you. . . . Okay, here goes. My mother and grandmother had been out weeding in my grandmother's lovely rock garden. I heard them say that they needed to do the front of the house next. I decided to surprise them and do it for them. I went out and cut down everything in front of the house. My grandmother cried for days.

What's your favorite childhood memory?
Catching fireflies in a mason jar in my great aunt's garden in Philadelphia. We let them go all at once in a cloud of light.

As a young person, who did you look up to most?
My grandmother, who was a wonderful storyteller.

What was your worst subject in school?
Math—I still have nightmares about skipping a math test, then missing the exam.

What was your best subject in school?
Literature—any course having to do with languages.

What was your first job?
In third grade, my sister and I (she was in second grade) started a newspaper. We kept it going for a couple of months.

How did you celebrate publishing your first book?
I honestly don't remember. I just felt as if I'd had a hit of laughing gas for about a month.

Where do you write your books?
In the office in my house.

Where do you find inspiration for your writing?
In other people's stories.

Which of your characters is most like you?
I think perhaps Mumtaz, Shabanu's daughter.

When you finish a book, who reads it first?
My husband, Wayne.

Are you a morning person or a night owl?
Both—I love both early morning and late night. I don't sleep a
lot.

What's your idea of the best meal ever?
A bucket of garlic crabs and draught beer at the Crystal River
Restaurant on the Gulf Coast in Florida.

Which do you like better: cats or dogs?
Ooooh! I don't want to choose. I like more dogs than cats—
but that's just because more dogs are people-friendly. The
cats I like, I like at least as much as my favorite dogs. (I have
three of each.)

What do you value most in your friends?
The desire to celebrate.

Where do you go for peace and quiet?
My husband I live in the country, where there is nothing but
peace and quiet. I'm more likely to go out looking for action.
There's a sandwich shop in the village down the road.
Sometimes, I take my newspaper there and have lunch.

What makes you laugh out loud?
When my dogs and cats play together in a jumble of ears
and tails.

What's your favorite song?
"Now the Day Is Over."

Who is your favorite fictional character?
Ratty from *The Wind in the Willows* for his many kindnesses
to Mole.

SQUARE FISH

What are you most afraid of?
Forgetting things I've promised to do.

What time of the year do you like best?
Spring.

What is your favorite TV show?
M*A*S*H.

If you were stranded on a desert island, who would you want for company?
My husband, Wayne.

If you could travel in time, where would you go?
I'd stay here. I love the suspense.

What's the best advice you have ever received about writing?
To excise everything that isn't absolutely essential to the story.

What do you want readers to remember about your books?
I want them to remember that keeping your mind open lets in a lot more light.

What would you do if you ever stopped writing?
I can't even imagine.

What do you like best about yourself?
I like it that I'm an optimist.

What is your worst habit?
Procrastinating.

What is your best habit?
Refusing to give up.

What do you consider to be your greatest accomplishment?
There are two. Running a marathon, and singing Bach's Mass in B Minor.

Where in the world do you feel most at home?
In a canoe or kayak.

What do you wish you could do better?
I wish I could sing beautifully.

What would your readers be most surprised to learn about you?
I have a deformed big toe from (1) tripping over a sidewalk in a pair of rubber boots, and then (2) having the same toe stepped on by a baby elephant.

SQUARE FISH

Keep reading for an excerpt from
Suzanne Fisher Staples's **The House of Djinn**,
available now in hardcover from
Farrar, Straus and Giroux.

EXCERPT

A small, slender woman with dark eyes stood near the edge of the roof looking out over the walled city of Lahore and reimagined her life. She had watched the seasons change over the red sandstone walls and the marble domes of the Badshahi Mosque for ten years. But this day she'd awakened knowing it would be the last morning of her old life.

Behind her, pigeons burbled and cooed softly to each other as they settled onto their roosts inside a room-sized wire cage in the middle of the rooftop courtyard. She let herself into the enclosure and picked up one of the birds, Barra, a proud old male who nestled his beak into the crack between her fingers.

The birds had belonged to Rahim, Shabanu's husband. After he was gone they were hers. In the old days, when the telephone trunk lines were undependable, Rahim had kept the pigeons to send messages back to his farm in Okurabad, about two hundred miles away. His most trusted servant, Ibne, kept another set of pigeons at the farm to return messages to the haveli in the city. Pigeons fly home with unfailing instinct, but they will not fly in the opposite direction. And so Ibne and Rahim transported the birds back and forth by truck. Later, when the telephone trunk lines were replaced by satellite signals, Rahim and Ibne continued to use the birds. They never tired of talking about them, comparing their speed and the color of their feathers: green for faithfulness, gray for speed, brown for strength.

Shabanu handled them every day when she fed them and changed their water and cleaned their cages. She stroked Barra's round gray head with the knuckle of her forefinger. The pigeon turned a pink eye on Shabanu, and his tiny heart fluttered against the palm of her hand.

Shabanu imagined words that might let her family know she was alive and well, that she would come to them soon. They must be words that would not expose herself and her daughter, Mumtaz, to her murderous brother-in-law Nazir. They must be beautiful words that would speak to her parents' hearts. Even as she contemplated the danger of sending them, she knew what they would be.

She stroked Barra's breast again and pressed her lips to feathers that shone pink and gray and green all at once before releasing him back into the enclosure. She shut the door to the cage behind her and walked past the parapet that overlooked the mosque and the Shahi Qila, the Old Fort adjacent to it.

Every day of her ten years on the roof of the haveli Shabanu had looked out at the fort and thought of Anarkali, who had been buried alive inside its western wall at the turn of the seventeenth century. The Mogul emperor Akbar had murdered the beautiful dancing girl whose name meant "pomegranate blossom" because his son had fallen in love with her.

When Shabanu had awakened this morning, her first thought was this: "You are living like the dead." Nothing had changed. She knew Nazir would kill her if he found her, just as he'd threatened to do after he'd killed his brother Rahim, and Shabanu had refused to marry him. But this morning she awoke knowing Nazir no longer had power over her. She tried to connect this thought to a dream, or a conversation she might have overheard from one of the rooftops across the way. But it felt more like a notion that had been swimming below the surface, circling like a primitive fish toward the light, waggling at her insistently, as if warning her not to ignore it.

Every night, from the realm of the buried, Shabanu dreamed of Mumtaz asking a child's questions, about where the stars went during the day, and why the shadow of the sun followed her wherever she went. There had been no one to answer these wonderings as her daughter grew. Now Mumtaz was fifteen, a young woman, and Shabanu imagined her with narrowed eyes that accused her mother of betrayal when she learned Shabanu had hidden herself away all these years. The heat of shame in Shabanu's cheeks was the most familiar sensation she felt when she thought of her daughter.

These ten years Shabanu had felt the absence of Mumtaz more keenly than she'd ever felt her presence. It was like a piece missing from the center of her heart where a mother's love should be.

The other greatest source of Shabanu's pain was that she'd left her mother and father growing old in the Cholistan Desert believing she was dead. She wanted to go to them, to ease their hearts, to see for herself that they were well. Sometimes it seemed her heart was made more of holes than solid parts, and that was her reason for sending the pigeon to Ibne. She had a physical need to see her daughter and to return to Cholistan.

Her days on the rooftop of the haveli were not so bad. Rahim's sister, Selma, who lived in the great old house below, visited her every day. Often they played cards at night, and talked over dinner. Samiya, a widow who was Selma's house servant and companion, joined them when she'd finished her chores in the kitchen.

Shabanu dreamed of a future in which she would return to Cholistan and teach the desert women to read so they could teach their children. She studied and she wrote poems and played her flute on the roof of the haveli, which stood a half story taller than the surrounding houses, so no one ever saw her. The poems were the letters from her heart that she couldn't send because no one could know she was alive. The flute music was her conversation with the world, expressing all of the wonder and hope she felt, despite her limited life.

Shabanu entered the summer pavilion, whose walls of carved marble screens had been her prison and her home. She crossed the stone-tiled floor to the low wooden desk where she had learned to read, and where she wrote and studied. Samiya had taught Shabanu and Mumtaz to read and write, first in Urdu and then in English. Shabanu sat on the floor cushion behind the desk and picked up the pen from the slot in its surface. She drew a sheet of the lightest parchment from the desk drawer and remembered the lines of a poem by the Sufi mystic Rumi. She wrote:

> *Flying toward thankfulness you become*
> *the rare bird with one wing made of fear,*
> *and one of hope.*

She folded the parchment, and refolded it into a square, then rolled it into a thin cylinder. She stood and returned to the pigeon enclosure. She closed the door and held out her hand. Barra landed lightly on her wrist. Shabanu talked softly to the bird and flicked the latch on the plastic capsule attached to Barra's leg. The lid clicked open. She threaded the parchment into the compartment and snapped the lid back into place. She stroked the pigeon's cheek once more and carried him to the edge of the roof.

Reaching both hands toward the sky, she released Barra. Immediately the bird's wings stroked the air, and he rose up against the red walls of the Shahi Qila. Shabanu's heart lifted as the pigeon, who'd been imprisoned on the haveli's roof for the same ten years, dipped, then soared as he caught the wind, his wings golden-edged in the sharpening light of morning. The last Shabanu saw of Barra was the iridescent green flash of his neck feathers as he rose against the red wall where Anarkali remained buried to that day.

Barra was an old bird, and had not flown any distance in a very long time. But he had been one of Rahim's best pigeons, and Shabanu believed he would fly for his home at Okurabad, faithful and mindless as an old retainer. Ibne would be there to open his cage. He would recognize Barra, and from the poem he'd know that only Shabanu could have sent him. Ibne and Rahim had shared a love of the Sufi poets, especially Rumi. Every evening one of them would recite a Rumi poem, and the other would reply with another. Shabanu learned them by heart before she could read.

Rahim had fallen in love with Shabanu when she was only a girl. She was on a ladder rescuing her cousins from a tree when he saw her first, and he was captivated by her flashing eyes. He'd never stopped loving her, although her family were poor, nomadic camel herders. Rahim sent Ibne as a go-between, bearing gifts of gems in small lambskin sacks for

Shabanu and her family. Ibne rode into the desert on a handsome white stallion, and he spoke to her parents with respect. Shabanu never loved Rahim and never wanted to marry him. But her parents had left her no choice, and he had been a good husband. She was certain Ibne would carry her note and read it to her parents in the Cholistan Desert.

Shabanu gazed at the sky beyond the minaret until long after Barra disappeared. And then she began to plan the rest of her day. Selma was going to visit her brother Mahsood, who had succeeded Rahim as tribal leader, for the afternoon and evening. Mahsood lived in a rambling old colonial bungalow across the city in Gulberg. Rahim always said his brother's house was haunted by mischievous djinn spirits: strange smells emanated from its interior, and lights appeared from nowhere, hovering menacingly before disappearing again. Rahim had seldom gone there. It was the house where Mumtaz lived, and Shabanu could bear the thought only because Rahim's nephew Omar also lived there, and she trusted him to protect her daughter with his life.

Selma wouldn't return until after a big dinner in honor of her niece Nargis and her family, who were returning to San Francisco after spending the summer in Lahore.

On this first day of her new life, Shabanu planned to slip out of the haveli while Selma was away and Samiya was busy, first in the laundry and then with shopping for groceries. Selma and Samiya were the only two people on earth who knew Shabanu lived on the roof. They had protected Shabanu faithfully these ten years, because they knew how dangerous Nazir could be.

Today Shabanu would hide herself within the billowing folds of a burqa and walk deeper into the old city to the bazaar, just to see what life looked like, this life that had been slipping past without her.

Shabanu waited inside the pavilion when she heard Samiya's quick knock at the door at the top of the stairs from the center courtyard below.

"I think the sky will turn itself inside out this morning," Samiya said. "I'm going to hurry with the laundry. Perhaps it'll dry before it rains." She set Shabanu's breakfast tray down on the table and poured tea. A glass of sweet lime juice, cloudy green and fragrant, and a plate with two onion paratha sat on the tray. "Would you like anything else?" Shabanu shook her head and smiled, and Samiya scurried out of the room, collecting Shabanu's dirty laundry from the basket at the back wall, outside the bathroom, as she went.

Samiya was just a few years older than Shabanu. She had worked as an ayah in the haveli across the lane. When the children were grown, Samiya had moved into Selma's house. She and Shabanu had become fast friends. Shabanu loved Samiya's birdlike quickness, her efficiency of movement and thought, her absolute loyalty, her sense of fun.

Shabanu heard the rhythmic thump of the washing machine down in the courtyard. She went to the trunk in her wardrobe and dug deep down to the bottom until she found the voluminous gray burqa that she hadn't worn since she took up life on the roof of the haveli. It smelled of mold and mothballs. Shabanu shook it out and laid it across her bed.

She imagined Samiya pulling the white sheets through the wringer that sat on the rim of the washing machine's tub, the sleeves of her tunic rolled above her elbows.

Shabanu took a deep breath and slipped the burqa over her head, adjusting it so the embroidered square through which she could barely see was in place over her eyes. Very little air seeped in, and Shabanu tried to steady her breathing to a low, shallow rhythm. In the damp monsoon heat, the musty cloth was almost suffocating, but she thought that freedom had never smelled so sweet.

Shabanu had learned to walk so silently on the rooftop it was a habit. Even she could not hear her footfalls as she crept down the stairs—only the occasional swish of the fabric of her burqa was audible in the narrow back staircase. She paused in the shadow of the doorway and listened for sounds from the courtyard. Samiya's sweet, high voice sang out from the laundry, and Shabanu crossed to the gate, fit the key into the lock, and turned it.

As she pulled the heavy gate toward her, its hinges screeched like a hawk flying low over the Cholistan Desert in search of prey, nearly stopping her heart. Instead of waiting to see whether Samiya would come running from the laundry, she slipped through the gate and relocked it, twisting the key until she heard the bolt slide home, then ran down the alley, her heart pounding.

She slowed to a fast walk as she rounded the corner at the busy thoroughfare that led into the bazaar. It was choked with handcarts loaded down with bolts of cloth being pulled by human beasts of burden, motor scooters spewing blue smoke from their exhaust pipes, donkey carts piled high with copper pots, shoppers making their way to the produce alley.

Shabanu wandered among the spice merchants, squeezing past great pyramids of amber powdered cumin and red ground chilies and green mounds of cardamom pods, breathing in the spice scents and listening to the bartering of shoppers and the profane banter of the shopkeepers. She watched ragged boys dart in and out among the stalls of the fruit vendors, stealing hard green amrud and shining red pomegranates.

She was intoxicated by the noise and dust and activity of the bazaar, more aware than she had been in ten years of the breath passing in and out through her nose and mouth, the steady beating of her heart, and the rushing of blood through her veins. It was almost as if she had been barely alive all that time, as if her body had put itself into a semi-conscious state of hibernation from which she was just now awakening.

She was careful to watch the time, and even so, barely made it home before Samiya came in from the market. She was asleep long before Selma returned from the banquet at Mahsood's house at Number 5 Anwar Road.

In the middle of the night Shabanu slipped back down the stairway to the gate and oiled the hinges so that the next day when she let herself out again it would sigh softly, just as she sighed going back to sleep.